STONEFACE

STONEFACE

AN ALLEN CAGE NOVEL BY
EDWARD R. JONES

DONALD I. FINE, INC.
NEW YORK

Library of Congress Cataloging-in-Publication Data
Jones, Edward R.
Stoneface / by Edward R. Jones.
p.   cm.
ISBN 1-55611-311-0
I. Title.
PS3560.04814S76   1991
813′.54—dc20   91-55184
CIP

Manufactured in the United States of America

10 9 8 7 6 5 4 3 2 1

Designed by Irving Perkins Associates

In memory of
H. N. "Swanie" Swanson.
How proud I am to have known you.

He to whom a watcher's doom
  Is given as his task,
Must set a lock upon his lips
  And make his face a mask.

—*Oscar Wilde*

CHAPTER ONE

The ability to extract innermost secrets from those de termined not to give them up requires an ingrained talent. You just can't teach such a thing. You can fine-tune your technique, maybe, become more proficient with your methods of persuasion. But the task of systematically reducing a vibrant, energetic Homo sapiens *to a heap of human debris, if necessary, takes more than mere technique. It takes an attitude, a vice-grip control over the pesky emotions and sensitivities that the human animal is burdened with ...*

At least that's more or less what Freeman McKee, in all unblinking seriousness, would tell Ben Hollister and John Malone during rare moments of introspection while stoned on good grass or otherwise consciously altered. On the occasional weekend when Ben Hollister's parents were away, Freeman would kick back on a couple of throw pillows in the big living room, gaze with disinterest at the latest adventure of Archie Bunker on the color TV, and relate these and similar weighty observations. Freeman considered himself an authority on the subject, because motivating people to part with such information was what Freeman McKee thought he might like to do for a living. He'd recently seen a slasher movie about a sadistic doctor who hired himself out to Third World countries to torture secrets out of political rivals suspected of plotting coups against the government, and the experience had struck a nerve. Seeing the good doctor's victims scream and writhe in unbearable agony had filled the boy with quiet excitement even at that tender age, and he thought that maybe he'd found his calling, if he could just figure out some practical way of making it pay.

Ben Hollister and John Malone, drawing from instinct and personal experience, readily acknowledged that he would probably be pretty good at it.

Of course, this wasn't a job description that Freeman would put on any resumé or talk openly about with only casual acquaintances. But he didn't mind discussing the topic with Ben Hollister and John Malone, because they'd grown up together in the Houston suburb of Spring Branch, sharing adventures and swapping lies and experiencing all the usual fantasies associated with adolescent male-bonding.

Except it didn't take long for his two cronies to realize there was something just a little peculiar about young Freeman McKee that stretched the boundaries of "normal" beyond credibility. Their first clue came a week after Freeman's eleventh birthday, when the three boys captured an armadillo in a fringe of desert just north of Interstate 10. At the time, eleven-year-old John Malone and twelve-year-old Ben Hollister were trying to coax the animal out of its armored shell, where it had withdrawn while being passed around by the frisky youths. But little Freeman had other ideas. "Let me show you how to get him out," he announced, and proceeded to roll the creature into a ball of desert weed, produced a disposable lighter, and turned the entire clump into a fireball. Ben and John had watched as the armadillo thrashed about inside the small inferno, neck and legs now fully extended, pinned to the ground with a forked stick held by the impassive eleven-year-old, who appeared unmoved. Minutes later, when it was all over, the smoldering critter lay motionless on its back, four blackened limbs pointing at the sky.

Freeman had lifted his eyes to his two shocked friends and said, "See? That's all there is to it. There's ways to make anything or anybody do what you want 'em to do. Usually all it takes is lighting a little fire under 'em."

After that, Ben Hollister and John Malone tried to ease away from Freeman, convinced that their young friend was a psychotic version of Dennis the Menace. But it was hard to do, because the truth was that Ben and John had become scared to death of the boy. They had suddenly discovered a secret look in the depths of those watery blue eyes that they'd previously construed to be bland innocence. Innocence, shit, the kid was loony as that maniac Charlie Manson. Would probably end up just like him. So common sense said to keep their distance and save themselves all the nightmares that would surely follow if they didn't.

Only they hadn't counted on Freeman McKee sensing his friends' wariness and, like all youths searching for their position in life's pecking order, delighting in his new role of intimidator. The more Ben and John tried to exclude him socially, the more forceful and insistent Freeman became. He continued to sit with them in the school cafeteria, carrying the conversation and ignoring their uncomfortable silence as they

3

exchanged glances and wished he would just go away.

In a further effort to shake him, Ben and John quit riding the bus and took to hoofing it the two and a half miles to and from school each day...only there was Freeman, trudging along beside them with a blank look on his face, chiding them softly for not letting him know. If they arranged on the sly to meet at the skating rink, lo and behold, there was Freeman, waiting for them. If they went to a Saturday matinee, the chances were great that all they had to do was turn around and there would be Freeman, munching Milk Duds and staring up at the screen with that porcelain face that had become such a big part of him lately. It was like the little sonofabitch had radar. And while Freeman had never been noted for his outstanding sense of humor, this new facial cast he had adopted was downright spooky. Come to think of it, they weren't sure they had ever even seen the guy *blink*.

But neither Ben Hollister nor John Malone had the nerve to come right out and tell Freeman they didn't want to hang with him anymore. They kept seeing and smelling that armadillo screaming like a tea kettle while being roasted alive, Freeman leaning into him with that forked stick...

No. The idea of telling Freeman McKee to take a hike had no staying power. And after witnessing what he did to Joe Odell in the boy's bathroom during recess one morning, they congratulated themselves on their judgment.

Joe Odell was only twelve, but his growth hormones had run wild, sprouting his frame past the sixty-nine-inch mark and weighing him in at about one hundred and eighty pounds. But as with many big men, nature had compensated for his size by giving him a mild disposition. Consequently the gentle giant wouldn't even participate in sporting events that involved the slightest risk of physical contact. In short, Joe Odell was a first-person wimp who had no desire to hurt or be hurt—which made him the perfect candidate for Freeman McKee's ongoing campaign to solidify himself as schoolyard rooster.

On this morning, Ben Hollister and John Malone were over by the urinals sneaking a cigarette with two other boys when Freeman came sauntering in, unreadable as ever. The entire school had heard about the armadillo incident, so an uneasy hush fell over the group as he stopped in the middle of the floor and made a production of wrinkling his nose, making sure he had everybody's attention.

"I smell pig shit," he announced, and looked toward one of the stalls. The door had a broken latch and was partially open, showing Joe Odell sitting hunched on the toilet with his pants down around his ankles.

Freeman walked over and pushed the door open all the way. Joe Odell, mortified at this invasion of privacy, looked up and said, "Huh?"

"I said add some water, I could smell you all the way down the hall."

Joe Odell sat there looking dumb for about three seconds before Freeman said, "Never mind, I got a better way," then took a half-step forward and slammed his knee hard against the big kid's face. The blow sent him sliding off the seat and onto the floor, blood streaming from a fractured nose and a stunned look in his eyes. Freeman reached down, took Joe Odell by his prominent ears, and began dunking his head into the murky water.

Freeman gave a final push and held the dazed kid's head under the surface with one hand while using the other to operate the flush handle. "I'll just flush it for you," Freeman said, "and give that ugly face of yours a mud pack at the same time."

The boys over by the urinals were rooted in their tracks, the two Pall Malls they were passing around now totally forgotten as they looked on in morbid fascination. Ben Hollister and John Malone thought it was the most humiliating and degrading scene they had ever witnessed.

Freeman had finally released the kid, who promptly curled into a fetal position at the base of the commode and began sobbing.

"Now everybody knows what a shit eater you are," Freeman said. And with that he walked out of the restroom without a backward glance, leaving Joe Odell's gut-wrenching sounds of agony echoing inside the heads of his subdued classmates, who were finding it very difficult to look at each other.

The next day, without explanation or goodbyes, Joe Odell left school for good. It was rumored that he had lost either the ability or the will to speak and had been placed in a private sanitarium outside Houston, but none of his former classmates wanted to check it out. What do you say to a guy who was forced to stick his head in his own shit?

After this, Ben Hollister and John Malone gave up their efforts to shake Freeman McKee. They agreed it was healthier that way. In their minds he had become the embodiment of the devil himself. No question about it, the crazy fucker definitely didn't have his grain stored in the right silo. He was capable of *any-*thing, including committing mayhem on nonagreeable school chums. And the worst thing about it was you never knew when he might go off, because you just couldn't get a make on what was behind that wooden-Indian expression.

"He's got a face like a fucking stone," John Malone told Ben Hollister shortly after the restroom experience. "You just can't get a register from him. They ought to put his head on a nickel or something."

"I got an idea," Ben had told him. "Why don't you go tell him his new nickname and let me know how he likes it when you get out of the hospital."

John said, "What nickname?"

"Stoneface. Fits him to a tee."

And thereafter, whenever the two boys were alone, they would make up "Stoneface" jokes and laugh at their cleverness, neither wanting to display to the other the stark fear that Freeman McKee had planted deep inside their souls.

Ostensibly, they became once again The Three Musketeers, inseparable chums who shunned all company except their own. In reality, Ben Hollister and John Malone were nothing less than pawns and court jesters, subject to the quiet will and unpredictable caprice of their younger companion...except that Stoneface never laughed. They were his minions, a constant ego booster to this new found power he'd come to enjoy. At the slightest hint of disagreement, all Freeman had to do was give them what they referred to as his "Medusa Look"—after all, she was the classic broad that turned you to stone if you looked at her—and all semblance of protest would die on their tongues. Freeman was justly convinced that his method of winning friends and influencing people was vastly superior to anything ever offered by Dale Carnegie. His was a tried and true system that had proved effective ever since the days of Genghis Khan. He'd read up on the man, admired his style. And what was good enough for Genghis was certainly good enough for Freeman.

Finally, three months before graduation, an agitated Ben Hollister cornered John Malone in the school library. "Look," he said earnestly, "we're gonna be living in paranoidsville the rest of our lives if we don't get away from that fucking Sphinx. Personally, I don't consider that a very enjoyable prospect, and I don't think you do either. Now we both know Freeman doesn't plan on going to college. He'll be lucky to finish high school. So I got me a brainstorm. Instead of staying here and going to UH, what say we put in applications to UCLA and move to California. Our folks can afford it. Let's face it, the only way we're gonna lose that psycho is by getting the hell out of Houston. *Way* out. Are you with me?"

John Malone, who by then was desperate enough to plead guilty to a felony if that's what it took to eliminate Freeman McKee from his life, had said with enthusiasm, "Man, let's *do* it."

They had a few anxious moments when they told Freeman about it later that night. Sitting in the front seat of Ben's Z–28 outside Bill's Barbecue, passing a joint and watching the hotrods cruising through looking for girls and a race. Freeman's reaction had been to take a long toke and hold it while he studied the tight rear end of the miniskirted waitress leaning into the window of the adjacent car. He let it out with a deep sigh and gave them each a look. "Keep in touch," was all he said. Then he had looked away again and that was the end of the conversation. Ben and John couldn't believe it had gone so smoothly. Stoneface would soon be history!

Ben Hollister and John Malone began their freshman year at UCLA with a whole new perspective on life. They moved into their own two bedroom off-campus apartment and began sampling the Southern California lifestyle. They loved the beaches, the nonhumid weather and year round tans. They loved the laid-back atmosphere, the nightlife that catered to all tastes, fantasies and social persuasions. They loved the opportunity of seeing their favorite movie stars up close and semipersonal if they cruised Rodeo Drive long enough. Ben Hollister even went totally Hollywood and had an ear pierced, stuck a ten-point zirconium in there out of admiration for Elton John, his favorite pop star.

But most of all, right up there at the very top of their list, they delighted in the fact that Freeman McKee was nearly two thousand miles away. At that distance he didn't appear nearly as frightening as he had when they were all rubbing elbows back in Houston. Now they could think about him from time to time when reminiscing and picture him as nothing more than a creepy caricature unworthy of serious reflection. Now they could *breathe*, spread their wings and fly with eagles instead of that psychotic turkey buzzard. Life was on the upswing, and Ben Hollister and John Malone had a vice grip on the pendulum.

They graduated together with the class of '86, looking smart and sophisticated in their black gowns and square caps. Ben, infatuated with the high-tech world of microchips, semiconductors and miniconverters, majored and excelled in electronics and Business Ad. John, not the mental equal of his friend, was content to concentrate on a career in physiotherapy. His goal was to be a trainer for a major league sports team. John couldn't play a lick of any kind of ball himself, but had always been captivated by the Michael Jordans and Bo Jacksons, who made it look so easy. He considered it a vicarious thrill just to be able to maintain that caliber of athlete humming on all cylinders.

Ben Hollister won the honors of being named class valedictorian, and he gave an impassioned speech about how the youth of America had unprecedented opportunities to revive the country's flagging high-tech component industry and give the Japanese a run for their money. Ben pointed out that eighty percent of new-age weapons systems—including the F–16 fighter, the new M1–A1 Abrams Tank and the Tomahawk Cruise Missile, all relied on guidance systems powered by microchips purchased from Japan. "In short," Ben said, "the effectiveness of many of our most advanced SMART weapons, both defensive and offensive, are solely dependant on those chips that can't be bought from anyone else." He had then paused for dramatic effect before leaning over the lectern and adding, "And let's not forget Hiroshima and Nagasaki, either. Because you can damn sure believe the Japanese haven't. And one day down the road we just might be called to task for that. And we'd better be ready."

Ben Hollister's speech was controversial to say the least, and an uncomfortable hush had fallen over the assemblage, more out of respect for the abundance of Japanese graduates in attendance than from any disagreement with his prophecy. But John Malone, sitting in the fifth row, said out loud, "Amen to that," and beamed at those around him as if he had just favored them with a particularly profound piece of insight.

Four years later, while working as an order analyst for the prestigious defense firm of TRW, Ben Hollister literally stumbled upon a new compound coating more resistant than silicon that increased the life and durability of ordinary microchips threefold. At the time he had been conducting experiments to test the compatibility of the firm's new Monel flow regulator with argon gas, making certain the combined elements of each wouldn't create a chain reaction that would blow the nuclear submarines it was designed for right out of the water. Instead of sharing the information with his employer, Ben decided to quietly patent the formula for himself.

Needing all the financial help he could get, Ben took the idea to his old homeboy John Malone, whose dreams of becoming a major league sports trainer had carried him as far as physical education director of a local Reseda junior high school. John, elated at being teamed up with his old school chum again, leaped at the suggestion, and they quickly put the bite on their parents, who also liked the proposal. Ben's father, a renowned architect whose firm had designed the magnificent Houston Oaks Hotel, had been especially impressed. "If you can do what you say," he told his ambitious son over the phone, "you'll corner the market in microcircuitry." To which Ben had confidently replied, "That's exactly what I intend to do. Will you back me?"

The old man did—to the tune of $350,000. John Malone's dad, a wholesale beer distributor, kicked in another $350,000 in exchange for a half-interest for his son, and the partnership was off and running. Ben Hollister hadn't been thrilled with the fifty-fifty deal, complaining to the old man that since it was *his* discovery, not John's, he should at least have controlling interest. But the old man had said take it or leave it, and Ben couldn't sign fast enough.

Back in California, they leased a large warehouse in Monterey Park and set up shop. They named the fledgling firm BenJohns Electronics, and in the first year alone they netted over a quarter million in profits—which prompted Ben Hollister to exchange the ten-point zirconium earring for a half-carat blue/white diamond.

During their third year, aided by a rush of media and trade-journal testimonials praising Ben Hollister as doing for microchips what Stephen Jobs had done for computers, they won a Secret clearance from the Defense Department and a seven-million-dollar contract from the Air Force.

Ten months later Ben moved into a three-point-two-million-dollar penthouse condominium in Marina Del Rey. John Malone, opting to go for the beach life, bought a small house in Pacific Palisades. He decided to have the interior completely gutted to accommodate his recent status and talked Ben Hollister into letting him move into the condo while the work was going on. Just so he could be close to the project, he said, so he wouldn't have to drive in all the way from Reseda. It wouldn't take long, he said, maybe five or six months. Ben, concerned with how the arrangement might look to their neighbors, reluctantly agreed.

He needn't have worried. This was California, where nothing short of gerbil-stuffing was likely to cause any raised eyebrows. The only time any of the residents ever saw them anyway was during an occasional trip in the elevator or while collecting mail from the alcove off the lobby.

As BenJohn Electronics grew, John Malone's role as functioning player had been reduced to attending weekly staff meetings and doing a little lightweight PR work. But mainly he collected his quarterly profits and stayed out of the way. John, though, was getting restless, he needed something to do with all this spare time. So he spent about eight grand on video and stereo equipment, turned his bedroom into a ministudio, and began filming a home-exercise video. Not only did it give him new purpose, but also offered the motivation of trimming the few extra pounds he'd allowed to accumulate over the years. He even bought a capuchin monkey and named it Rasputin, because he thought it looked just like a small hairy monk in a nun's habit. Rasputin would keep him company while he rehearsed his routine for the camera, wearing a black neoprene body glove zipped open to the navel that showed off his well-proportioned one hundred and sixty-five pound body. Carefully positioned stage lights would glisten softly off his lightly oiled skin while he stretched and twisted, soft rock playing in the background . . .

It was also during this fourth year that an incident occurred that catapulted the two men into a heightened state of awareness and put them in touch with their own vulnerability. It was just after 3:00 A.M. on a Sunday in May. They'd come home from a Z.Z. Top concert at the Forum, a little high, and there, sitting on their living room sofa, was a shadowy male figure. His features were hidden, the only lighting coming from the fifty-gallon aquarium against the back wall, but he acted like he belonged there.

Ben Hollister stopped dead in his tracks and stared in amazement. "What the . . . who the hell are you? How did you get in here?"

"Now is that any way to greet an old buddy?" the shadowy figure asked, and Ben Hollister and John Malone went into instant sobriety. They didn't need light to realize their uninvited visitor was none other than their old boyhood nemesis Freeman McKee. That toneless drawl was as familiar to them as was that death-mask face they had lived with for so long. Then he had leaned forward and looked up at them and their worst nightmare was confirmed.

"I thought I asked you to keep in touch," he said.

CHAPTER TWO

Brenda Alworth put the caller on hold and said to Allen Cage sitting at the desk across from her, "Is there any way we can install a home security system *today?*"

Cage looked up from the message slip he was reading, then glanced at his watch: 8:20 A.M. "Depends on what it is," he said. "Who wants to know?"

"A man named Ben Hollister. Highly agitated too, I might add." She frowned at the phone in distaste. "To quote him ... 'I don't give a rat's ass what it is, as long as it does the job and gets in today.' Some people really have a way with words. Line one, if you want to talk to him."

Cage picked up the phone. "Mr. Hollister? My name's Allen Cage. I understand you want an alarm system installed today."

"You told that shit right," the voice on the line said. "Can you do it?"

Brenda was right, Cage thought. The guy sounded

stressed-out and desperate, like he'd reached the end of his rope. Another one of those domestic things, probably, somebody wanting to make sure an ex-lover didn't sneak back in and make off with the hidden coin collection.

Cage said, "I'll need a little information first, Mr. Hollister," and reached for pad and pen. "Are we talking about an apartment or a house?"

"It's a penthouse condo in Marina Del Rey," the voice said. "The Ocean Colony. What else?"

Cage went on full alert, thinking this was serious money here. His paycheck could certainly use a little commission bonus right about now. He said, "How many points of entry, like doors and windows?"

There was a pause on the other end, then the sound of an exhaled breath. "Man, I got twenty-six hundred square feet here. Split level, four bedrooms, combination den/library, wrap around balcony. I got windows in the living room, I got windows in the den, I got windows in the bedrooms, I got a window in the kitchen and one of those small square doors that covers the trash chute—does that count? I don't *know* how many goddamn windows I got, I never stopped to count 'em. Now if you can't help me out, say so, 'cause I got to find me somebody fast who can. Jesus, is business that good?"

"These are dangerous times we live in, Mr. Hollister."

"You're telling me. Look, why don't you just come on out and check the place yourself. I'll pay you for your time even if it don't work out. Just make it quick, will you?"

"What's the address?"

"Two-seven-o-twelve Admiral Way. Just ring PH–2 and I'll buzz you up. It's supposed to be a security building, but you couldn't prove it by me." He hesitated, then said, "Allen Cage, huh? I know that name from somewhere. Ever done anything newsworthy?"

"It doesn't take much to make the papers, Mr. Hollister. I'll see you shortly."

Cage hung up the phone and saw Brenda giving him a questioning look, fingers poised above the keyboard of her computer. Everyone at Banes and Twiford called her Olive Oyl, a nickname that stuck because of her mild resemblance to the cartoon character— tall and lean, with large dark eyes and waist-length black hair that she kept braided in dual ropes. Though she lacked in glamor, the three men were nevertheless quick to agree that Brenda Alworth had been blessed with the sexiest female voice that ever came out of a telephone, a quality that had more than once tipped the scale in favor of Banes and Twiford when bidding against competitors. Paul Banes was fond of telling her that she could make a fortune in the Dial-A-Porn trade.

"You disapprove?" Cage asked.

"I don't disapprove," she said. "I'm just wondering how you're going to install a security system today all by your lonesome. Paul won't be back from Hawaii for another eight days, and Larry won't be finished with 20/20 Video until tomorrow."

"The guy lives in a hi-rise condo at the Marina, Olive Oyl, a penthouse. That might eliminate having to wire any windows. In which case we only have one point of entry to protect, the front door. If so, then a coded entry box with auto-dial would probably do the trick. I could do that in under six hours."

"And pick up a nice three-eighty in commission while you're at it."

"What's wrong with that? I can use it. Caprita's

birthday is next week and I wanted to rent a cabin cruiser and take her over to Catalina for the day. Maybe now I can do it."

"Why, Allen Cage, I didn't realize you were so romantic."

Cage pushed back his chair and stood up. "I'm doing it in self-defense. We had an argument last night and now she's not talking to me. Which reminds me, will you give her a call and say I'll be a little late getting home? She'll be at the hospital by now."

"Can I tell her about Catalina too?"

Cage was headed for the door. "Why not, you tell her everything else I do. Be a shame to break tradition."

"That's because we want to keep you out of trouble, dear," Brenda said, and reached for the phone. "After all, we know you."

The Ocean Colony was one of those towering structures of glass, steel and concrete that seem to spring up like mushrooms around luxury yacht clubs and posh marinas catering to the mega-rich. This one was designed in a half-moon configuration that cradled two tennis courts and an Olympic-size swimming pool, and offered each unit an unimpeded view of the expensive pleasure boats bobbing gently in their slips.

Cage eased his Mercury Cougar into a parking slot marked VISITOR, then walked to the callboard outside the double glass lobby doors and buzzed PH–2.

Through the intercom: "Who is it?"

"Allen Cage, Mr. Hollister."

"You see anybody else hanging around out there? Like a short stocky guy with curly brown hair and a face like a hockey mask?"

Cage gave the area a cursory inspection, thinking

someone had really given the man a bad case of the frights. "Nope, nobody like that down here. Just some lady walking a white poodle."

"Mrs. Cranepoole," the voice said. "Come on up. But don't let anyone in behind you."

The door buzzed and Cage entered, crossed a burgundy-carpeted lobby and took an elevator to the eighteenth floor. He followed the arrow to PH–2 and pushed the chime-bell that was sunk into the middle of the heavy mahogany door.

It was opened immediately by a man wearing a silver New Balance warmup suit and a diamond earring. He was about thirty, average build and height, with thinning blond hair and puffy eyes. He needed a shave. But it was his harried expression that was most notable, the loose folds of skin around his mouth pulled into deep frown lines that gave him the appearance of being in mourning.

"Mr. Cage," he said, "I have a feeling you're gonna be my salvation. Come in, come in."

"Call me Allen," Cage said, taking the extended hand.

"Let's keep it even. I'm Ben."

Ben Hollister led the way through the living room, down a short hallway and into the den, talking all the while, occasionally looking over his shoulder to make sure his salvation was still with him.

"I really appreciate you coming out here like this, Allen. I know you guys probably got plenty of work, what with the crime situation being what it is and all. Damn shame, you know it? Folks have to button their homes up tighter than Fort Knox to even stand a chance of feeling halfway safe. Whatever happened to the good old days when a man could stay gone all day and not even lock his door?"

"They went out with the Gold Rush of 1849," Cage

said. "It's been all down hill ever since."

"Ain't that the truth? And I don't think it's gonna be long before we *all* reach bottom. Here we are, grab yourself a seat. Right there on the couch is fine. You want a drink or something?"

Cage sank down onto the brown leather sofa. "No, thanks, I don't drink."

"Well, I sure do," Ben Hollister said. "I haven't slept a wink all night and I need a little high octane to keep me going."

He crossed the room and went behind a wet bar built into an alcove beneath a curved staircase leading to the second floor. He removed a quart of Wild Turkey from under the bar and a tumbler from the glass shelf next to the sink and poured a full measure. He raised the tumbler to his lips, careful not to let any spill over the rim, tossed it back with a quick motion and stood squeezing the glass with his eyes closed until it hit. Ben Hollister shuddered, brought the tumbler down hard on the genuine cherry-wood bar and looked at Cage.

"Ahh! Now I can *talk* to you."

He came around the bar and settled onto a matching love seat across from Cage, propped his white Nikes on the heavy glass coffee table and sighed. "I guess you figure anybody starts hitting the bottle at nine o'clock in the morning's got a problem, huh?"

Cage, his voice neutral, said, "What's the difference? Nine in the morning or nine at night, the effect's still the same."

"Well put. Maybe you ought to go into PR work. Do I hear a little South in that accent?"

"You do. North Carolina. Haven't been back in a while, though."

"I thought so. Pretty country down there. I'm Houston born and raised, myself. Me and my partner both.

Who I'll introduce you to if he ever gets his ass out of that bedroom. He's making a work-out video, and I'll be go to hell if he ain't training a *capuchin monkey* to work out with him. Thinks it would be a good gimmick to have the thing bounce up and down on his washboard stomach, or something."

He craned his neck around and yelled at the top of the stairs, "Hey, John, get down here, will you? Want you to meet the man who's gonna solve all our problems." He turned back to Cage. "He loves that monkey. Named it Rasputin."

Cage said, "I haven't promised anything yet, Mr. Hollister . . . Ben."

"I know," Ben said confidently, rubbing his hands together and surveying the room. "But I'm positive you can come up with some way to help a fellow Southerner out of a bind. You want to look around a little, see what we got? Start right here if you want. The French doors lead out to the balcony, as if you can't see that for yourself. It wraps all the way around the corner to the kitchen and dead ends against the stairwell housing. We got four bedrooms and two baths upstairs. I still haven't counted the windows yet, but I guess you can do that."

Cage pretended not to notice how nervous the man was, the way his Nikes kept waving at him from the coffee table. If success in life was judged solely by status and personal comforts, then Ben Hollister probably qualified as one of the city's new movers and shakers. But right now it was Ben Hollister who was moved and shaken, and Cage was curious about what had set him off. Long money didn't scare very easily.

Cage said, "Ben, has your security here been breached lately? Because if that's the reason you're so set on having an alarm system installed today, it would be a big help if I knew how entry was made."

"You're damn right it's been breached," Ben said. "Last night—or rather early this morning—John and I are coming back from a Z.Z. Top concert. We get to the livingroom and find this guy all reared back on the couch like he's part of the furnishings. You realize what a shock that is, place like this? I mean, you think you're immune to that shit and pretty safe from intruders, right?" Ben Hollister dismissed the idea with a snort. "Bull *shit*. If he'd had a gun he could've shot us both where we stood before we even knew he was here. Tell me I don't need an alarm."

"Did you call the police?"

"No," Ben said, and looked away, scratching his elbow.

"Did you notify building security?"

"What building security? All they got is a geriatric doorman, and half the time you can't find him 'cause he's down in the garage nipping Thunderbird with the maintenance man. And the only thing management cares about is selling the four empty units they got. We should've bought a townhouse."

"Any sign of forced entry?"

"He picked the deadbolt and shimmed the knob latch with a strip of plastic."

"How do you know?"

"Because he told me and showed me," Ben Hollister said. "He wanted me to know how easy it was."

He skewered around on the love seat, checked the top of the stairs again, then turned to Cage. "Look, why don't you just go ahead and make your inspection and meet me back here when you're finished. I'll explain the rest to you after I get John down here."

Cage went out on the balcony first, following it past the curved ceiling living room, on past the formal dining room and around the corner of the building to the kitchen. He paused next to a potted orange tree to look out over the railing at the marina. It was a perfect day, warm and bright, with just enough of an ocean breeze to keep the smog away. Down below, the wharf was coming alive with boaters scurrying around in shorts and sneakers, looking small and insignificant from eighteen stories up. He saw a brunette in a blue bikini being helped aboard a sixty-foot Hatteras by a sunburnt and wrinkled old man wearing white duck trousers pulled up to his rib cage. The woman's hair and compact shape reminded him of Caprita—which in turn reminded him of their argument the night before. She was probably stalking the corridors of Wilshire Memorial right now, going about her duties as charge nurse, tight-lipped and silent, brushing her hair out of her eyes with impatient gestures the way she always did when she was angry. He was secretly hoping that Olive Oyl would tell her about Catalina. Maybe she'd get a case of the guilts and tell him it was a sweet thought but that dinner and a movie would be sufficient. He could manage that for less than a hundred. Cage told himself he wasn't being cheap, just prudent. Making up was supposed to be fun without costing more than a full week's paycheck in the process. Caprita would understand that, she was sensible. Most of the time, anyway.

Oh, well, if he was able to do this job, he'd have more than enough to swing the boat trip and try to get Caprita in a better mood to accept his sound arguments. So he'd better get to it.

Cage pushed away from the railing, took pen and spiral notebook from his inside jacket pocket and began examining the balcony.

*   *   *

Cage said, "Okay, here's what we're dealing with."

He was back in the den, sitting in a wing chair this time, legs crossed and notebook opened on one knee. Ben Hollister, nursing a fresh drink, was on one end of the sofa, and the wiry guy Ben had introduced as his partner John Malone was on the other. John had his capuchin monkey with him. It was perched on the arm of the sofa nibbling with jerky motions at a stalk of celery—not eating it, just chewing it into pulp while he gazed at Cage.

"You've got a total of fourteen points of entry," Cage said, "including the three sets of French doors off the den, living and dining rooms, and a sliding glass door off the kitchen. I'm particularly concerned about the kitchen area, because the stairwell exits onto the half-roof right above it. Besides that you have eight windows—four up and four down—as well as the front door and utility door in the kitchen. Each of those points will have to be hard-wired to your telephone lines."

Ben Hollister said, "So what does all this tell us?"

"It tells us that no way can I hook up any kind of alarm system today. And neither can anybody else who's conscientious about their work."

Cage waited for a response. All he got was a grunt and the clinking of ice cubes as Ben took a long pull from his Wild Turkey and Seven-Up, set the glass on the coffee table and said, "Well, I guess that's that, huh?"

He didn't sound as disappointed as Cage would have expected. Probably just worn out.

"Two days minimum," Cage said, "three at the outside. That's what we're looking at on installation. Believe me, no one wants to take care of your security needs more than I do, but I have to be realistic. Oh, I could stick a piece of crap in here in a few hours that would look and sound impressive as hell, and with your opportunists that would be good enough. But it wouldn't stop a pro for two minutes, so I'd be doing you a disservice."

For the first time since their introduction, John Malone spoke. Cage thought he saw a mild resemblance to Madonna's ex, Sean Penn, except Malone dressed a lot better. While Ben Hollister's preference leaned more to the hip/trendy side, earring and all, John Malone was a model of contemporary/cool. He wore charcoal gray cotton slacks with pleats that looked sharp enough to draw blood, and a powder blue silk shirt buttoned all the way to his protruding Adam's apple. He had thick brown hair combed neatly to the side and a smooth, lightly tanned complexion that gave him a wholesome schoolboy appearance.

"Well, at least you're honest about it," he said. "But that isn't gonna solve our problem, is it? I don't know how much Ben's told you, but we had a little incident here last night."

"I *told* him already," Ben said, irritated. "You think I wouldn't tell him?"

"I was just making sure. Personally, I think we should have called the police, but Ben here thinks that's a bad idea. He thinks we're still kids and have to bow to the schoolyard bully."

John Malone didn't act very pleased about the course of action they'd chosen.

Ben Hollister gave Cage a helpless look. "John's got this thing about image," he said. "He's worried we'll look like wimps, hiring somebody to keep the boogie man away. He doesn't understand that the most important part of image is prudence."

"In case you hadn't noticed," John said, "Ben fancies himself a philosopher."

Ben Hollister took his Nikes off the table and leaned

closer to Cage, ready to talk serious.

"Let me tell you a little something about this guy," he said. "His name's Freeman McKee. John and I grew up with him back in Houston. He loves to hurt things. We saw him take a kid who outweighed him by at least sixty pounds and stick his head in a shitty toilet. Held it there while he flushed it. He actually convinced another kid to let him break his wrist, saying the kid could claim he slipped on some wet steps and sue the school for negligence. Know how he broke it? Twisted the kid's arm up behind his back, then slowly bent his wrist backward till it snapped, the kid screaming like a banshee. Freeman acted like it was some kind of an experiment or something . . . kept watching the kid's face the whole time and never so much as blinked an eye. Is that cold?"

"Sounds like a nice guy."

"Oh, that's not all of it by a long shot. I'm just giving you examples."

"We left Houston eleven years ago just to get away from this guy," John Malone said. "He used to talk about how much of an art form it was to know just how close to death's door you could lead a subject without actually sending him over. A *subject*. The guy's a real spook. Now the spook's back again, popping up like Jason in a *Friday The 13th* sequel."

"We called him Stoneface," Ben said, swirling the ice cubes in his nearly empty glass. "But never to his face."

Cage was becoming fascinated with Freeman McKee. "Since you already know him," he said, "why not just call the police and file a B&E or unlawful entry complaint?"

"We don't want him sitting a few miles away in the L.A. County Jail," Ben Hollister said, "we want him out of Los Angeles period."

"Did he make any threats? Any demands?"

"Not in so many words. Said it had been a long time, and since he was in the neighborhood he thought he'd stop by and see how we were doing. He looked around, said we had a real nice place, so we must be doing pretty good. The whole conversation didn't last five minutes and he sounded like a recording. Wants us to meet him at Kelbo's restaurant at eight tonight to do a little reminiscing and discuss our future. Like he was our business manager."

Cage had the feeling Ben was leading up to something that had nothing to do with alarms. The way he kept shifting his eyes to John Malone, who was pointedly ignoring him now.

Cage closed the notebook and put it back in his jacket pocket. "I can understand your concern, Ben, but I don't know what else to tell you. Except to go ahead and meet the guy and see what he has to say."

"I got a better idea," Ben said, peering at him over the rim of his glass. "Why don't you go in our place?"

"Excuse me?"

"Go in our place. Be our emissary, so to speak."

"More like our bodyguard," John Malone mumbled.

Whenever John Malone spoke, Cage found his eyes drawn to the monkey instead of the man. It was kind of disconcerting. Rasputin was clinging to the guy's neck now, John having to bob and weave to keep the animal from poking him in the ear with that stringy piece of celery.

"This isn't escort work," Ben said, and gave John a hard look. "It isn't bodyguard work, either. All we're asking is you meet the man at Kelbo's, see what's inside that fucked-up head of his, then tell him we're not interested. I'll give you five hundred dollars right now, cash, check or credit card. Easiest money you'll ever make."

"I see. You want me to play the heavy and try to intimidate a guy who gets off on breaking bones and dunking people's heads in toilets. What makes you think I'm qualified to do that?"

John Malone stroked Rasputin's furry head and said, "I told you he wouldn't do it."

"John, will you please shut up and let the man mull it over? ... Okay, Allen, I'll tell you why I think you're qualified. Remember I told you on the phone I knew your name from somewhere? Well, a big part of my business involves communications, so when we hung up I called my research department and had them put you on the computer. It wasn't twenty minutes before they called back with a complete printout of a story the *Times* did on you last year." He flashed Cage a large smile and tugged at his earring. "Hell, guy, you're famous. Or would *in*famous be a better word?"

Cage had tagged Ben Hollister as a man who liked the sound of his own voice. He would be a conversational tyrant at social gatherings, the type who would stand in the middle of the room with a drink in his hand and tell war stories without letting anyone else get a word in edgewise. About all you could do was grunt and nod in the right places while you looked for a reasonable excuse to get the hell away from there.

Cage wanted to do exactly that. He had enough paper work back at the office to last him most of the day. But the man had offered him five bills just to meet with this guy and tell him in no uncertain terms to get lost. What would that take, maybe an hour? Wouldn't hurt to think about it a little more, now that his commission was gone. Especially since the man had gone through all this trouble to impress him.

Ben had one arm draped over the sofa back, studying the vaulted ceiling. "Let's see now. Used to own a small carnival, didn't you? Back in '81 or '82, I think. You were doing a show in Escondido and decided to go across the border and do a little shopping in Tijuana. On the way back they found an ounce of grass in your car and charged you with trafficking."

"It was a half ounce," Cage said, "and it had been in my glove compartment for two weeks. I just flat forgot about it."

Ben focused on Cage. "Oh, I believe you. But you came in right at the beginning of that Zero Tolerance bullshit and ended up with two years fed time. Normally the story would end right there. You do a year, maybe fourteen months, and they parole you. But you couldn't wait that long, could you? You escaped from what, nine prisons all together?"

"Seven." Actually it had been eight, if he included Nicaragua. Which he couldn't, because only a handful of government people were supposed to know about it.

Ben winked at him. "What the hell, after the first half-dozen, who keeps score, right? The point is, you beat seven federal prisons, and that, I'd say, shows determination and ingenuity and guts. But what really floors me is this FBI agent going to bat for you. Got you out on parole, didn't he?"

Ben was talking about Larry Twiford, and he'd done just that. Larry had been special agent in charge of the Raleigh, North Carolina, field office at the time Cage had made his final escape—from the Atlanta Federal Prison in Georgia. It was Larry who ultimately arrested him five months later while he was having breakfast at a Howard Johnson's on I–40 just north of Greensboro. After becoming familiar with the case, Larry decided Cage had gotten a raw deal on the pot bust and mentioned his circumstances to a superior in Washington. That conversation resulted in Cage being spirited out of a maximum-security prison in Illinois and sent to Nicaragua—only to be deliberately arrested in that country so as to gain access to Nicaragua's notorious Tipitapa prison. The reason? To escape with another American prisoner the U.S. government wanted a lot more than they wanted Allen Cage.

The whole thing had been mind-boggling, but Cage agreed to give it a try when told that success would get him out of prison. It hadn't gone exactly as planned, but the results earned him an unconditional parole. Shortly after his release, Larry Twiford resigned from the Bureau and opened a private security firm on Santa Monica Boulevard with his brother-in-law, Paul Banes. Larry had offered Cage a job, saying that anybody who could break out of seven maximum security federal prisons had to be an asset to any security company.

Make that eight, he reminded himself again.

Cage said, "Most people wouldn't consider escaping from prison to be an endorsement for the kind of work you have in mind."

"To the contrary," Ben said. "It shows you got balls as big as Texas and don't know the meaning of quit. I'll take that over a routine tough guy any day. So, will you do it or not? I'll pay you right now."

Cage had done some considering while Ben had been talking. At 8:00 P.M. he'd be on his own time, not company, so he'd have a clear conscience there. What the hell, even cops moonlighted.

And he could sure use an extra five hundred.

"Cash okay? You don't have to report it."

"A check will do," Cage said. "And, yes, I do have to report it."

"Great," John Malone said tonelessly, and swung

the monkey up on his shoulder, where it grabbed a double handful of hair and bared its teeth at Cage. "Let the games begin."

Ben gave his partner another look, then beamed at Cage. "That's it then," he said. "You might have noticed John and I have a slight disagreement on how to approach this thing, but I kind of won out. I figure rather than go to extremes, it might be more prudent to let Freeman know we're not interested in renewing past acquaintances, if you get my meaning. I'll trust your best judgment on how to get the point across."

"I'll try to see he gets the message," Cage said, then asked Ben Hollister how he'd be able to recognize Freeman McKee.

"The face. You can't miss it. Clean-shaven and round as a full moon, not a crease in it, and wide blue eyes that seem to be interested in everything. And that's the way it stays, never changes regardless of what he might be thinking or feeling. You'll know him when you see him."

"Alright, I'll talk to him. But you're hiring me, not Banes and Twiford. And I do nothing illegal. Fair enough?"

Ben raised his glass. "Any way you want to handle it."

"As long as we have an understanding. Now, does this mean you aren't interested in a security system?"

"Hell, no," Ben said. "Make Freeman McKee see the light and I'll take the most expensive system you got—within reason—and take all the time you need installing it. Is that an easy sale, or what?"

CHAPTER THREE

It was ten after six when Cage pulled into the driveway behind the small apartment complex on Camden Avenue in West L.A. and eased the Cougar into its carport slot next to Caprita's white Volvo. He collected his fresh dry cleaning, crossed the driveway and entered through the patio gate of Apartment Two.

Caprita, wearing red shorts and one of his paint-speckled blue shirts knotted around her middle, was using a sprinkle can to water the jungle of plants and flowers she had arranged along the inside of the high wooden fence. She glanced at him, then went back to her watering, a sign of dismissal.

"I thought you were going to be late," she said.

Yep, she was still pissed.

"I love you, too," he said. "And how was your day?"

Caprita emptied the sprinkle can without further comment and stalked through the patio door and into the kitchen. Cage followed and draped his clean slacks and dress shirts over a table chair. He moved to the sink where she was washing her hands and began to lightly massage her neck. She stiffened but didn't pull away.

"Look at you," he said. "Tight as a drum back here. Let me work these kinks out and we'll start again."

Caprita whirled around and placed her hands against his chest. "Oh no you don't, you're not pulling that cheap psychology on me. Next you'll be saying it's PMS. I have a right to be upset and you know it."

"Why? Because you want a baby and I'd rather wait? Don't my feelings count too?"

"Now you're twisting it, Allen. Poor boy, you're so misunderstood. Bullshit! The reason I'm furious with you doesn't have anything to do with whether or not you want a baby. It's because you refuse even to *discuss* the subject and tell me *why* you don't want one. Is it because we're not married? I know how terribly traditional you can be."

Traditional. That was one of Caprita's diplomatic synonyms meaning stubborn and old-fashioned.

"We don't need a piece of paper telling us it's okay to have a baby," Cage said. "And I *did* tell you why. I told you at least twice that—"

"—you weren't ready. And that's *all* you've told me. Are you not ready mentally? Are you afraid you might be an abusive parent? Is it financial, global warming, the general instability of the world? What is it *specifically*, Allen, that's all I want to know. Then maybe we can deal with this thing on an even basis."

Cage went to the refrigerator, opened it and began pawing through the shelves, looking for a can of Seven-Up. He found one and popped the top, stood there taking small sips while he tried to figure out how to explain it to her. Parenthood was a state of mind, either you were geared for it or you weren't, and right now he wasn't. But not for any of the reasons Caprita had mentioned.

She said, "Well?" and leaned against the sink with her arms folded beneath her small breasts.

"I don't mean to put you off," Cage told her, "but this isn't a real good time to go into it. I've got a meeting at Kelbo's at eight o'clock and I have to shower and change. Don't worry about any dinner for me."

"See what I mean? Anything to dodge the issue. Well, I'm not going to be sidetracked this time. I'll be thirty next week, Allen. You're thirty-eight. You don't have to be a biology major to understand that time is definitely not on our side. So you tell me here and now when *would* be a good time and pencil me in. I mean it, Allen. I want to know where the stumbling blocks are."

She turned back to the sink and began scrubbing her hands under the running faucet. Back in her silent mood now, the rigid arch of her back telling Cage that this was not over yet.

"Alright, then," he said, "how about tonight? I should be back nine, nine-thirty tops. We'll make some mocha, sit right here at the table with no TV or distractions, if that's how you want it, and I'll tell you exactly what bothers me about it. How's that?"

"Fine."

"Now will you stop being mad at me?"

"Go take your shower, Allen," she said quietly. "We'll talk tonight."

Caprita waited until he left the room, then turned off the water and dried her hands on a paper towel. No point in cooking now. She put the fresh chicken from Lucky's in the freezer and decided a tuna salad would be fine for her. She went about making it and reflected on this growing strain on their relationship.

She didn't consider herself a very demanding person. But having a baby was an emotional tug that was gaining in strength with the passage of time, and she was finding it harder to deny it. But it took two and she needed Allen's cooperation. At least that was the better way. Oh, sure, she could toss away those damn pills in the medicine cabinet and come home one day shouting, "*Surprise.*" Tell him it must have been an act of divine providence. He would reel for a few days but he would accept her word without question and learn to adapt. Eventually he might even be pleased.

No. She would never try to trap him that way. It had to be his decision. But she had to admit that if she'd known of his reluctance about becoming a father before falling hopelessly in love with him, she might have reconsidered.

That had been eighteen months ago, in Nicaragua of all places. She'd been a volunteer nurse serving in an ill-equipped hospital on the outskirts of Managua, part of an increasing number of American activists who believed the U.S. was financing an immoral war in that country and who were donating their time and skills as their own form of protest. She'd been an idealist then, a dreamer who believed that sacrifice and commitment could make a difference.

Then she'd met Allen Cage in the lounge of the Intercontinental Hotel and her priorities had taken a drastic change. He looked out of place, this tall pale man hunched over the bar deliberately drinking himself into a state of oblivion. Which hadn't taken much, since she'd learned that, other than an occasional glass of wine, he never touched alcohol. His look of sadness and disillusionment had captured her maternal instincts, and she had amazed herself by striking up a conversation. Only later did she learn the shocking truth—that the FBI had taken him from a maximum security federal prison in the U.S. and transported him to Managua in order to be thrown into *their* prison in an effort to escape with a huge man with red hair who had hijacked a shipment of deadly nerve gas in North Carolina and somehow ended up in Nicaragua. The end result had found them sprinting up the coast to Ensenada, Mexico, aboard a thirty-six foot cabin cruiser with a six-foot-seven inch madman who was determined not to let them off alive. Five days of near constant terror, surrounded by nothing but open water with no place to run or hide.

Caprita felt her heart racing just thinking about it as she sat down to eat her salad. She should have gotten some kind of assurance from Allen before they agreed to move in together, find out how he felt about having children. But she had been freshly in love at the time and it didn't seem so important then.

But it did now. Did that mean the freshness was wearing off? She didn't think so. She loved him as intensely now as she ever did, she was certain of that. But what would she do if he flatly refused to ever become a father? Would she stow away her need in some unused cranny of her mind and live the rest of her life in stoic silence, an unfulfilled martyr for love? Or would her desire become so great that she would one day stow away her feelings for Allen and search for a more suitable prospect?

By the time she'd finished her tuna salad and placed the dishes in the dishwasher, she was forced to admit that she still didn't have a ready answer to that question.

She was curled on the livingroom couch watching Hard Copy when Cage came out of the bedroom, dressed and smooth-shaven and smelling of Aramis, her favorite men's cologne. She thought he looked boyish and eager, with his curly brown hair glistening damp at the ends, long legs and slender hips fitting comfortably inside black dress Levi's. Like a good-natured country boy on his first night in town. But Caprita knew how deceptive that appearance could be.

He paused to tuck in his shirttail, gazing at the TV. "The *National Enquirer* of the airways," he said. "They juice up every story they do."

Caprita said, "So tell me about this meeting tonight."

"Somebody I have to talk to on behalf of a client. Well, officially he's not a client yet. So far he's only hired me to meet with a guy tonight and deliver a message, because hopefully he's gonna be leaving town tomorrow."

"Isn't that a little odd?"

"It's a lot odd, but there are what you might call extenuating circumstances involved. It's a long story. Anyway, I won't be long."

He kissed her cheek and headed for the kitchen.

Caprita said, "Allen?" and waited for him to turn. "I really don't want to go to Catalina on my birthday. It's sweet of you, but that's also my day off, and I don't feel like spending it on a boat."

Cage grinned. "Olive Oyl couldn't wait to tell you, huh? Can't keep anything secret around that woman."

"And you well know it too, don't you?" she said, and grinned back, formally breaking the ice.

"Hey, I would've taken you," he said defensively. "But since we're back on the subject and Catalina's out, what *would* you like to do?"

"Conceive," she said.

CHAPTER FOUR

Kelbo's is located at the junction of Pico and Gateway Boulevards in West Los Angeles. It's one of the oldest eating establishments in the city, noted for its excellent seafood, "World Famous Barbecue Ribs" and potent tropical drinks. It's easily recognizable by the attached artificial thirty-foot lighthouse and contrasting stained glass windows. Inside it's a seafarer's dream, with gurgling aquariums, fish-net ceilings and strategically placed ship lanterns for atmosphere. Ancient marine relics are everywhere, including an old diver's suit just inside the entrance with a painted face peering out through the helmet.

Cage stood next to the diver and let his eyes adjust to the dimness. A dark-haired woman in a green silk dress approached and gave him a cherry-red lipstick smile.

"Table for one, sir?"

"I'm meeting somebody," Cage told her. "About thirty, doesn't smile much. Anybody like that come in lately?"

The woman nodded. "I know the gentleman. I believe he said there would be two joining him?"

"The other one couldn't make it."

"Follow me, please."

She led him past the crowded bar to a row of booths in back separated by tall partitions that screened the occupants from view on three sides.

"The fourth booth," she said. "I'll send your waiter right over. Enjoy your dinner."

Cage moved slowly down the line, passing an elderly couple slurping their way through steaming bowls of clam chowder—on past a family of three, the mother struggling to restrain a bucking two-year-old of indeterminate sex in a highseat while dad scowled at the menu—past two chicly dressed women in their early forties who ceased talking in whispered tones and looked up from their cappuccinos with mild interest as he went by and stopped at booth Number Four—

And looked down at Freeman McKee, the man he had come to meet. Sitting facing him in the middle of the booth, attention focused on his dinner of filet mignon and Maine lobster, apparently oblivious to anyone else's presence.

Cage did an instant analysis of the man and concluded that whatever he did, he did well. He wore a light gray worsted suit that Cage had seen advertised in Caprita's recent edition of Vanity Fair with a price tag of twelve hundred bucks. Deep purple silk shirt with a narrow white collar, a perfect Windsor knot in the dark striped tie. He had a black onyx on his right pinky and a flash of heavy gold peeking out from under his left pearl cuff link that logic dictated had to be a Rolex.

But it was the man's face that threw Cage. Despite Ben Hollister's description, he'd built up this mental image of a rectangular slab of concrete with tight mouth and hooded eyes. But this face was indeed as round as a new moon and smooth as porcelain, topped by a full head of brown hair that curled lightly over small, flat ears. An ageless face devoid of laugh wrinkles or worry lines, a hint of purple beneath striking blue eyes that indicated he might suffer from insomnia. With a little imagination, Cage thought the man looked an awful lot like an early version of his favorite movie star, Rod Steiger.

It took maybe five seconds before Freeman McKee raised his head and asked pleasantly, "Do I know you?"

If this guy was a native Texan, he'd sure worked at losing the accent. His voice was low and measured, without any hint of geographical origin.

Cage said, "No sir, I don't believe you do. My name's Allen Cage and I'm here to represent two acquaintances of yours who you wanted to meet with tonight. Ben Hollister and John Malone?"

The man hesitated a moment, apparently conducting his own analysis while slicing off a wedge of filet and forking it into his mouth. "Let me see your driver's license," he said.

"What for?"

"I want to see if you gave me your real name."

Cage pulled out his wallet and flipped to the plastic window showing his license. He pointedly covered his address and social security number with his thumb and held it out for the man to see. Freeman McKee leaned forward and studied it, chewing slowly. After a moment he leaned back and said, "Sit down, Mr. Cage."

Cage took a seat and immediately a waiter appeared, handing him a menu, asking if he wanted a drink. Cage ordered a Seven-Up and the waiter left.

Freeman McKee had returned to his dinner. Without looking up he said, "Steak's a little chewy, but the lobster's top-notch."

"I'll bet it is," Cage said, "but lobster isn't in my food budget this month."

"My treat," Freeman said.

"Thanks, but I'll pass. Think I'll take advantage of this Kelbo burger and fries while I have the chance. I need some honest to God calories."

Their waiter was still hovering in the background. Cage signaled him and gave his order, telling him to hold the dill pickle. The waiter left again and Cage turned back to Freeman McKee. The man was looking at him, now and again blinking in slow motion like he was about to nod off, those wide baby blues focused on a point just above the bridge of his nose. It was, Cage knew, a practiced effort, creating the illusion of direct eye contact while actually avoiding it. You could listen to a guy tell his whole life's story without being moved either way.

"Who are you, Mr. Cage? And why are you here?"

Cage had already decided on the straightforward approach. He folded his arms on the table.

"Well, seems like you put quite a scare in your old friends, popping up like you did last night. Tell you the truth, they're a little frightened of you."

"Why should they feel frightened of me? They're my friends."

"You know how it is. People sometimes build up unreasonable fears about other people's motives. Especially if they have money and status."

"I have money and status. And I don't have any fears."

A warning, though Cage couldn't detect any change in the man's voice, certainly none in his expression.

"I'm sure that's true, Mr. McKee. You strike me as

a successful man who knows what he wants and how to get it. What line of work are you in, if you don't mind my asking?"

Freeman McKee dipped a wedge of lobster into the lemon butter. "In other words, my old homeboys won't even have dinner with me after not seeing me in eleven years. I'm hurt."

He didn't look hurt. He didn't look anything.

Cage said, "Well, you *did* break into their condo, Mr. McKee. I guess their concern comes from the fact that old friends don't normally come calling that way."

Freeman bit into the lobster wedge and chewed while he again focused on that spot between Cage's eyes. "Those boys always did overreact. Even when we were kids. Blowing things out of proportion. Just like now."

He shook his head once and looked away, as though unable to believe it, then back at Cage. "I come into town, unexpected, on business, decide to pay a visit to a couple of boys I was really tight with, invite them to dinner, and they sic you on me. Do you work for them, or just freelancing?"

Cage spread his hands. "You didn't answer my question."

"What if I told you to get fucked and mind your own business?"

Cage shifted his own gaze to a point just above the bridge of Freeman's nose. "Let's hope it doesn't come to that."

Cage was silent while the man drank the rest of his wine and wiped his mouth with a clean napkin. "Don't worry, Mr. Cage, I can take a hint. Tell your guys I apologize for any stress I put them through and won't bother them again. My business here will only take a few days and then I'm gone. I don't want any trouble."

"Well, now, I'm sure they'll be real glad to hear that. Thank you for your cooperation."

The waiter came then with his burger and fries, complete with the giant dill pickle that he didn't want resting on a bed of cole slaw. Nobody ever remembered to hold the pickle. He asked the waiter for another Seven-Up and reached for the ketchup, aware of his hunger, saying, "I'm gonna enjoy this."

Freeman McKee dropped the napkin on the table and slid out of the booth. "You'll excuse me, Mr. Cage, but I have an important phone call to make back at the hotel. I think everybody understands everybody now."

He fished a wad of bills from his pants pocket, peeled off a fifty and dropped it beside his plate. "That should cover both meals and take care of our man. It's been interesting talking to you."

"Likewise," Cage said. He started to rise and shake hands, but Freeman was already buttoning his jacket and walking away. The man obviously didn't believe in lingering goodbyes.

Cage dug into his burger and fries. That hadn't been so bad. He had to admit that Ben Hollister and John Malone had him going there for a while, with all those war stories about the guy. *Stone*face? *Moon*face would have been a better description. About five-foot-nine but heavy through the shoulders and chest. The beginnings of a gut resting on his belt buckle. He was just arrogant enough to make asshole status, but Cage could see no real evidence of the monster his new clients had made him out to be. Freeman McKee might have been right; his old schoolmates had probably let their imaginations run away with them and overreacted.

Still, you never knew. Everybody had at least a small piece of themselves they'd rather keep buried, that never got added into other people's perceptions. Look close enough, though, and most would give up a glimpse of this secret side during unguarded moments. Then there were others with such rigid control that they never showed you anything at all . . . until it was too late. Freeman McKee just might be of such a breed. Might even be dangerous. But whatever the man was deep inside, Cage hadn't been able to pin it down. Unless it was something so alien as to be outside his experience. And that would take in an awful lot of territory.

The waiter came over and asked if he'd like anything else. Eyeballing the fifty next to Freeman's plate, daring to dream that it might be his tip.

"Just fix up the tab and take everything out of that," Cage said, nodding at the fifty. "What's left is yours."

The waiter renewed his fading smile, took the fifty and disappeared.

Cage found the telephone in the little alcove outside the restrooms. He put a coin in, removed a business card from his shirt pocket and dialed a number written on the back.

Ben Hollister must have been waiting by the phone because he answered on the first ring. "Well?"

Cage said, "What if it had been somebody else calling you?"

"I'd have hung up. How'd it go?"

"On the surface, no problem. Said he was in town on business a few days and decided to drop in and say hello. Said he apologized if he caused you and John any—to use his word—stress. Said he wouldn't bother you anymore."

"You believe him?"

"Hard to tell, you know him better than I do. He sounded like he meant it."

A pause on the other end, then: "How did you come

on to him? Hard-nosed or Mister Niceguy?"

"I appealed to sweet reason. I also let it be known I wasn't just making a request."

"Freeman McKee's never been reasonable in his life. Burglarizing people in the middle of the night, that sound reasonable to you?"

Cage said, "Has he ever lied to you?"

Another pause. "Now that I think about it, I can't recall him ever doing that." He seemed to perk up a bit. "You know, I think maybe you did convince him. He always did like to shock people, keep 'em off balance. *Could* be that's what he was doing last night. I'll give it three days, Allen, and if we haven't heard from him by then you got yourself another five bill bonus and a debt of gratitude. How's that sound?"

"That isn't necessary," Cage said. Then, not wanting to appear stubborn, added, "But I appreciate it. What about the alarm system?"

"Same deal. We don't hear from him in three days, I'll take the best one you got. You said it would take about that long to install it anyway, didn't you."

"That's right."

"So we're on then. I'll call you in three days. Thank you again, Allen. I mean that. Take care."

Click.

Cage held the phone to his ear for several moments before slowly hanging up. Then he allowed a wide grin and stepped lively all the way out to the parking lot and his Cougar, his mood considerably brighter than when he'd arrived.

Freeman McKee, waiting in the rented Dodge Spirit parked in the back row of Kelbo's, didn't know that the maroon Cougar parked third from the end belonged to Cage. He had to lean across the seat when it became obvious the man was going to pass right by his front bumper. Walking with his head down, fiddling with his keys, feeling pleased with his performance.

Like it was really going to be that easy.

Freeman heard a car alarm being deactivated. He raised his head to window level and looked out. There he was, getting into the Cougar. Taking his time leaving. He would have already called Ben and John and given them his report. Little trembling pricks, neither one of them had the heart of a June bug. And here he hadn't done a thing to them at all.

Not yet.

The Cougar's engine and headlights came to life and Cage went past him again, made a right onto Gateway and stopped for the light.

Freeman followed, easing out of the parking space and down the driveway with his lights off, waiting until the Cougar caught a break in traffic and made another right onto Pico.

Freeman hit the lights and accelerator and fishtailed out of the lot, spewing gravel and cutting off a shiny red Corvette that had to break sharply to keep from running up his tailpipe. He nearly broadsided a shuttle bus as he swung onto Pico and fell in half a block and three cars behind Cage, leaving a symphony of horns in his wake. He zeroed in on the Cougar's taillights.

Freeman was feeling one of his moods coming on, which affected his stomach juices. Who did this clown Cage think he was anyway? He *did* act like a pro. Not volunteering any unnecessary information, covering the address on his driver's license so that he now had to waste time following him home. What was that cute bit? *Let's hope it doesn't come to that.* Well, hang on to your wig, Mr. Allen Cage, because it is coming to that. First he'd find out where the guy lived. Then he would decide the punishment.

Freeman turned his thoughts to Ben Hollister and John Malone, and his stomach churn picked up a notch. Success had made those boys bold, caused them to forget the teachings of their youth. He hadn't left a good enough impression. An oversight that would have to be remedied before his business here was finished.

A flash of red on his left caught his attention. It was the Corvette he'd cut off coming out of the parking lot at Kelbo's. A big kid in his early twenties behind the wheel, dark hair pulled back in a tight ponytail. He came roaring up alongside Freeman and slowed, rolling down the passenger window, screaming at him.

"Cocksucker, you cracked my goddamn windshield doing that shit! Pull your ass over!"

Freeman had his window down and heard him clearly but gave no indication of it. He was fixed on the Cougar ahead, not wanting to get too close so that the guy might spot him or too far back and get caught by a light.

The kid was still screaming. "Motherfucker, did you hear what I said? Pull *over!*"

The Corvette had to brake for slower traffic and fell behind. Freeman, still riveted on the Cougar, hardly noticed. Cage was nearly a full block ahead of him now, signaling to get in the left lane. Freeman slowed and hit his own signal, but as he made his move to change lanes, here came the red Corvette again, zipping up on his left and hanging there, temporarily hemming him in. The kid was still screaming obscenities and ordering him to pull over, threatening to kick his ass at the next light.

In the meantime Cage had moved into the left lane

and increased his lead to more than a block. Freeman accelerated, wanting to pull in ahead of the Corvette, but the kid easily kept pace, refusing to give way. He was going to cause Freeman to lose the Cougar, which was now slowing to make a left turn at the second intersection.

Freeman backed off the gas then and for the first time gave the kid his full attention, both cars now doing about twenty-five as they approached a signal light. The green still favored them, but Freeman could tell by the flashing DON'T WALK sign that they were about to see a red. The kid saw it too, and his mouth twisted into a triumphant smirk as Freeman watched him release his seatbelt and hunch forward, concentrating on the light, the kid's movements saying that he just couldn't wait until they came to a stop so that he could pound this geek into the pavement. Traffic was starting to line up behind them now, nobody able to pass as the signal changed from green to orange to red.

The kid in the red Corvette came to an abrupt halt, set the hand brake and reached for the door handle. "*Now*, motherfucker—" and saw a long black cylinder poking out at him from under the man's arm that was resting casually over the window frame. Recognition dawned, and for an instant the kid was frozen. Enough time for the black cylinder to make a minute adjustment before it sounded once. The kid's head snapped sideways as he went limp and slumped against the door, a small hole above his right eyebrow.

Freeman tucked the .22 Ruger target pistol with threaded silencer back between the seat and console and waited for the light to change. He did not look at the kid again, knowing it wasn't necessary, but redirected his attention to the Cougar that was just now making a left at the next intersection. The light turned green and Freeman pulled away at a sedate pace, moving into the left lane that was now wide open for him, gradually picking up speed and barely making the left turn arrow before it went red. He glanced behind him and saw the red Corvette still sitting at the light, a string of vehicles playing musical horns backed up for almost a block.

Freeman was through the intersection and again searching for the Cougar, his stomach on full tilt. He spotted it up ahead, moving with traffic, and relaxed a bit. He took a pack of Rolaids from his coat pocket, popped two in his mouth and crunched them thoroughly before swallowing, feeling the coolness slowly extinguishing the flame in his gut. He would be fine in another minute or two. It always went away shortly afterward. Sometimes he had to beat it down with a mental stick, but ... it always went away.

He settled back and continued following the man in the maroon Cougar. He would not lose him. Allen Cage might just as well be on a leash.

Allen found Caprita in the living room, curled up on the couch in her long pink robe, her tabbycat Grits on her lap. Waiting for him with New Age on the stereo and two sandalwood scented candles on the coffee table. Ready for their heart-to-heart talk.

She looked up. "How was your meeting?"

"It was alright. Let me change and I'll be right back."

"I'll be here," and blew a kiss.

Cage went into the bedroom and took off his clothes, slipped into gray sweatpants and blue robe and went into the bathroom to brush his teeth. Staring at his image in the mirror while he tried to come up with a credible argument against having a baby that Caprita would at least understand. She wouldn't be impressed by generalities; she would expect him to defend his position with specifics. Only he couldn't do that. But she would be prepared, ready to spring at the first flimsy excuse he gave and tear it apart with indomitable logic. So he'd have to be cautious and watch out for loopholes. Otherwise she'd box him in so tight that any rationale he offered short of sterility would sound frivolous. Caprita could get misty-eyed over a legitimate sob story, but let her sense insincerity and she'd go straight for the testicles. In this case, literally.

He rinsed, dried his hands and went back into the living room. Caprita had brought out her heavy ammunition; a bottle of Cabernet Sauvignon, the only form of alcohol Cage would drink. The problem was that one glass was all it usually took to make him congenial enough to accept anything she said. She knew that. It also made him horny. She knew that too.

Cage sat down beside her and eyed the full goblet on the coaster in front of him. "You're not playing fair," he said. "You don't want a discussion, you want a surrender."

"I'll take any advantage I can get," she said, and shooed Grits off her lap and onto the floor, where he stretched lazily and ambled off toward the kitchen to check out his bowl. Caprita picked up her glass and held it up to him. "To us," she said seriously. "May the happiest days of our past be the saddest days of our future."

Cage lifted his glass to hers, took a sip and put it back on the coaster. "Where'd you get that? Has a nice ring to it."

"Three years ago, at a girlfriend's wedding. The

groom said it just before they cut the cake. It only came back to me this minute."

"See? There's something to be said for marriage after all."

"They're divorced now."

He said, "Oh," and reached for his glass.

Caprita twisted around to face him, giving him a flash of smooth inner thigh as she tucked one slender leg beneath her. "That's what really bothers you about this baby thing, isn't it? That we're not married. Regardless of how much you deny it, that's what you're hung up on."

"And I keep telling you that's *not* it. Oh, I could say it was and make a damn good case for myself on a compromise. You agree we get married, I agree we have a kid."

"That's not compromise, that's extortion. What could we gain from buying a piece of paper from the state and paying a preacher to pronounce us man and wife? You notice it's man and *wife*, not woman and *husband*. To me that signifies obedience to the husband. That's another word that was commonly used—obey."

"I believe nowadays they say husband and wife," Cage told her. "What difference does it make anyway? We can make up our own. Anything we want to say."

"Oh, Allen, it isn't about vows. Can't you see? It's the insti*tu*tion of marriage I'm talking about. There's something about it that makes people different, that tends to turn relationship into ownership. We have a great relationship. Why fuck with fate?"

Cage said, "Uh huh," and took a slow sip of wine, watching out of the corner of his eye as she bristled at the nothing remark.

"What does *that* mean? Uh huh. Are you patronizing me?"

"No. Just not agreeing with you. You're leery of this institution called marriage because all your life you've operated as an independent. You're a born activist at heart, babe, getting involved with protest groups like CISPES and spending months of your life doing volunteer work in Third World countries like Nicaragua. It gives you a purpose and satisfaction, makes you feel *better* about all the advantages you had being raised by wealthy parents because you at least tried to give something back. Nothing wrong with that. It's admirable. But you've been married to causes so long that right now you're in no hurry to marry anything else. At least that's the way I see it."

It was a long speech for Cage. He shut up and drank some wine and listened for a moment to the instrumental harmony from "Celestial Soda Pop" filtering through the hidden speakers. Beginning to feel mellow and philosophical, the smell of sandalwood and Caprita's perfume pleasing his nostrils, the low candle flames creating interesting shadows and impressions around the room. This was pretty good wine. A few more swigs and he'd be ready for Willie Nelson and Ray Charles doing "Seven Spanish Angels," joining in on the chorus the way Caprita did whenever she heard Whitney Houston doing "One Moment In Time." He wasn't sure how he sounded, but she couldn't sing a lick.

Caprita lifted her hands and let them fall into her lap. "I don't believe it. I'm letting you bamboozle me again. We were *supposed* to discuss your reasons for not wanting a baby, and you go bending the subject back to my not wanting to get married. You keep saying it doesn't matter, and yet you keep bringing it up."

"And it doesn't matter. But it's relevant. We both want the other to do something that neither of us is ready to do right now. I'm not insisting that you marry me. You shouldn't insist that I become a father."

She gave him an incredulous look. "That's not the same thing at all and you know it. Damn it, Allen, all I'm depriving *you* of is a document with my signature on it that wouldn't give you any benefits you don't already have. You're depriving *me* of a big need that I only have so many years to fulfill."

Cage hadn't looked at it that way before. He set the wine glass down and adjusted his position, stalling for time, then decided to just level with her. Either she would understand or she wouldn't. Whatever, she had that much coming.

"It's because I'm jealous," he told her. "And selfish. You wanted the truth, there it is."

"What do you mean?"

He had to choose his words carefully here. "Remember on the boat coming back from Nicaragua? When it looked like Red was gonna kill us both?"

She nodded. She had relived the event over and over in her mind for nearly eighteen months now. At one point she'd even considered counseling to stop the bouts of terror that would seize her unexpectedly and send her into uncontrollable shivers. Only they were forbidden to speak about it to anyone.

"I've never been so scared in my life," he said. "Because you were the first thing I'd ever really loved since I was eleven years old, when I lost my parents in a car wreck. I couldn't stand the thought of anything happening to you too. Even if I was going with you."

He could feel the wine now, loosening his tongue, draining his soul.

"I told myself if we survived, I was gonna spend the rest of my life catching up on all the years when I didn't have you ... or someone like you. I had so much giving stored up inside that sometimes I could bust with it. Then you came along and there was my outlet and suddenly I was on top of the world, lighter than air. That was a year and a half ago and nothing's changed. I want to be with you every minute of every day and every night, and if you think I'm exaggerating you're wrong. You're like everything I ever wanted and like nothing I've ever known and I don't want to share you with a baby. Not yet."

Caprita looked down at her glass, gently running her index finger around the rim. Momentarily at a loss for words. What could she say to such a testimonial? She knew that Allen loved her, but this was the first time he'd ever shown his real emotions. His words had been straightforward, eyes holding a silent appeal for understanding as he stripped away all the camouflage and laid himself bare for her.

She looked up and studied his profile as he stared at the blank screen on the console TV across the room. He had a nice one—strong jaw, high cheekbones and a ruler-straight nose. She would often tease him by saying he looked just like Thomas Jefferson on the head of a nickle, only without the wig.

He turned back to her and caught her smiling. "What's the grin for?"

"I was thinking about when I dragged you up to Portland to meet my folks. Their only daughter goes trekking off to Nicaragua on a peace mission and comes back with an ex-con fresh out on parole. I thought mom would die when I told them about you ...as much as I could. But daddy was on your side after hearing the whole story."

"He wasn't so much on my side when you told him we'd decided to live together. As I recall, his exact reaction was, 'What? without getting married?' Then you go, 'Oh, daddy, this is 1990, times have changed.'

Meanwhile I'm wanting to slide under the dinner table and stay there till you two finished discussing me."

"They finally came around, didn't they? Now they're your biggest supporters. And they want *grand*-children, Allen. Married or not."

Cage slid down and put his arm around her, brought her into the nook of his shoulder. "Tell you what," he said. "Give me another six months to get used to the idea, then we'll give it a go."

She pulled back and searched his face. "You mean it?"

"I mean it. Barring poverty or disaster. Will you work with me on that?"

She snuggled back under his arm and nuzzled his neck. "You know I will. Thank you, Allen, that's all I wanted." She moved to his ear and nibbled at the lobe, pressing against him with an impish grin. "Feel like going through a dress rehearsal?"

Cage was watching Grits meander into the living room, licking his lips and looking for something to rub against. "You're shameless, you know it?"

"And you love it," she said, lowering her eyes to his lap. "Don't you?"

"Like maple syrup and country ham, babe," he said, and gave her a squeeze ... then tensed as he brought his attention back to Grits. The cat had been massaging itself against a leg of the coffee table, its belly full and back arched. Now it was in a heightened state of alert, crouching near the end of the sofa, ears laid back and its gold-flecked eyes round with intensity as it stared at the blinds covering the window above the fish tank.

Something, or someone, was out there.

"Gonna get a couple of aspirin," he told Caprita, then got up and moved casually into the kitchen. He went straight to the cupboard above the sink and got a two-foot long rubber-handled flashlight that with batteries and all weighed a good six pounds.

He slipped quietly out the kitchen door and through the patio gate, then down to the corner of the building, where he paused to get a good grip on the flashlight and the creepy feeling that was in his stomach. The meeting with Freeman McKee had revived old instincts, caused him to leap at shadows. Still, it didn't hurt to be careful.

He peered around the corner, flicked on the flashlight and directed the brilliant beam down the side of the building, sweeping the low shrubbery and neatly arranged flower beds outside the row of apartment windows.

Nothing.

He walked to their living room window, parted the shrubs and put his face to the glass. There was a small space at the lower left where the blinds didn't quite fit flush with the sill. Cage squinted through the opening and saw Caprita on the couch, lighting a Marlboro with her battleship Zippo. He'd forgot to mention that. If she wanted a baby, she'd have to give up smoking. He'd insist on that.

He stepped back from the window and turned the light to the carport across the driveway, probing the dark shadows between vehicles where the overhead lights didn't reach, lingering on the Cougar and Caprita's Volvo parked side by side . . .

Still nothing.

Okay, so he might be off-center and a little lightheaded from the wine. Caprita would kid him about it, tell him a bird had landed on the sill, or maybe one of Grits's girlfriends had come lurking around. So why did he have this sensation crawling up his spine like someone was about to tap him on the shoulder?

Cage went back inside, leaving the patio light on and double-checking the deadbolt.

Caprita was in bed, lying on top of the covers in nothing but white cotton panties that contrasted well with her natural dusky complexion inherited from her Spanish great-great-grandfather. She was using the remote to scan the forty channels on the small TV.

"Where did you go? I missed you."

"To get a breath of fresh air. That wine made me sleepy."

"Not too sleepy, I hope." She found a repeat of "Cheers," put the remote on the nightstand and slipped under the sheet. She wriggled around for a moment, then brought her hand back into view holding the white panties. She dropped them on the carpet and patted the empty space beside her.

Cage got out of the sweatpants and robe, moved to his side of the bed and slipped in beside her, shrugging off his uneasiness. He switched off the nightstand lamp and turned to her, the glow from the TV highlighting her body in interesting ways as she draped one leg over his middle and began playing with his chest hair.

"You want to spend every minute with me, hmm? That's very romantic but it would get old pretty fast. But I loved hearing you say it anyway."

She kissed him then, long and slow and wet and sweet. Cage lay still and let her lead the way, tasting her lips and inhaling the afterscent of bubble bath. Content for the moment to lie there with his eyes closed and try to anticipate her moves. Her hand glided lightly over his chest and then down to his stomach, leaving a trail of goosebumps behind that sent tremors all the way to his brain.

She pulled back and gave him a somber look. "I love you, Allen," she said. "There'll always be a space

inside reserved just for *you*, where no baby or anything else will ever intrude. You're not the only one
who has a lot to give."

Then she was kissing him again, nibbling at his
nipples and stomach, sending the shallow muscles
into spasms, and he thought for perhaps the hun-
dredth time how great they were together.

Like maple syrup and country ham.

Freeman McKee gave it another minute after he saw
the light from what he believed was their bedroom
go out, then stepped from behind the dumpster at the
end of the carport and stared at the darkened window,
the play of flickering shadows on the closed blinds telling him they had the TV on.

The cat had given him away, and this Allen Cage
character had picked right up on it. Freeman had been
crouched beside the living room window, squinting
through the slit in the blinds, and had seen it in the
man's eyes—the way they had narrowed and gone on
instant alert as they went from the cat to the window
and stared dead at him without realizing it. Then
trying to play it off by acting nonchalant, saying he
needed some aspirin. He knew the man was going to
check it out. He knew it because he would have done
the same thing. He was beginning to think that he
and Allen Cage were a lot alike.

In some ways.

He stood quiet in the shadow of the dumpster and
watched the bedroom window. They would be fucking
now, he'd bet on it. A sweet gentle fuck with lots of
cooing after that bullshit cry-in session they just had
where the cunt had manipulated him so beautifully,
using her pussy like a weapon the way they all did.
She wasn't a bad looking little split-tail, though, if

you liked them fresh and wholesome in a Sally Field sort of way.

He was still smarting from the guy's attitude in Kelbo's and had been tempted to go ahead and take the man when he came sneaking out. Just slip the Ruger from his waistband and pop him while he stood there flashing that floodlamp all over the place. Eliminate any potential complications. But that would be too easy and wouldn't satisfy his sense of retribution. Freeman dearly loved hardcases. They were the ones who hurt the most when their egos were destroyed. And then the rest of them.

First, though, he had to take care of business. That was top priority, what he was getting paid for. He would take his real pleasure after the job was done.

Reluctantly, but with great expectations, he turned away and went back to his car.

It would start soon, now.

CHAPTER FIVE

Freeman McKee had left Houston two months after Ben Hollister and John Malone made their hasty move to California. True to Ben's prediction, Freeman never even considered college but drifted south, eventually coming to roost in Miami with a single suitcase and twenty-three dollars in his pocket. Besides clothes, the suitcase also contained his dad's army issue .45 Colt Automatic that he'd sneaked from the old man's dresser drawer before leaving. Life was filled with hidden perils and he never knew when a little heavy firepower would come in handy.

It was the gun that first got him in trouble and at the same time assured his future.

His first priority after reaching Miami and stowing away the suitcase in a Greyhound locker had been to replenish his finances. With the .45 tucked out of sight beneath his tan safari shirt, Freeman went in search of something to rob.

But first he needed a drink to take the edge off, so

he flashed his altered ID that said he was twenty-two at a bored barmaid and ordered a seven-seven. It was while he was putting the wallet away that he unknowingly exposed the butt of the .45 peeking out from the small of his back. A cocktail waitress heading for the bar-station with a tray full of glasses spotted it and immediately told the manager. Freeman got his seven-seven. Ten minutes later, after two no-nonsense Miami cops came up behind him and ordered him to put his hands flat on the bar, he got a quick trip to the Dade County Jail.

They booked him for carrying a concealed weapon and conveying a loaded firearm into a public drinking establishment. The latter was a misdemeanor and no big deal, but the former was a felony that carried a max of five years in the slammer, so the judge refused to release him on his own O.R. and set his bond at twenty-five hundred dollars. Since Freeman was classified a transient, no bondsman would risk underwriting him even if he could afford the ten percent fee. So Freeman was remanded to jail pending a preliminary hearing to be held three weeks later.

They put him in a tank for youthful offenders so he wouldn't get raped by the hardasses. The tank was designed to hold fifty-six inmates under the age of twenty-one. When they ushered Freeman through the gate with a fresh bedroll after court-call that evening, the count was ninety-three. The four-man cells were long since full, and newcomers were issued foam pads to flop on wherever they could find space on the concrete floor. Freeman had taken one look around and wished he was back in his old two-man holding cell. There were only three available spots left that he could see—two over by the row of toilets at one end of the dayroom, and one directly underneath the color television mounted in a wire-mesh cage at the other.

In between were two long metal picnic tables bolted to the floor, where half a dozen assorted card games were in progress.

Freeman headed for the space under the TV, stepping over and around half-naked bodies propped against the tank bars engrossed in torn girlie magazines and dime store novels. But before he could get there he was intercepted by a squat, heavily tattooed Hawaiian kid named Benny Taupua who was generally accepted as tank boss by virtue of the fact that he stood five-feet-eight inches tall and two-feet-four inches wide and could whip anybody's ass in there.

Benny had placed a hand in the middle of Freeman's chest and said, "Where you think you're goin', brother?"

"To find me a place to sleep."

"You mean that nice clean spot under the TV where you can hear all the programs real good?"

"That's the one."

"That's mine," the Hawaiian kid had said. "You can have it for a box of cigarettes. Camel regulars. Either that or you drop your gear back there by the shitters and catch all that good aroma."

Freeman had seen the kid in the back cell when he first came in, stretched out on the bottom bunk with a new Hustler held at arm's length, admiring the centerfold.

"I don't have any cigarettes," Freeman told him. "Don't use 'em."

"Pay me Thursday," the Hawaiian kid had said. "That's commissary day."

The racket had fallen several decimal points as other inmates became aware of the confrontation and paused to see what happened. Freeman, inexperienced in the ways of jailhouse etiquette, was nevertheless well-versed in the art of intimidation, and he handled it like a pro. The Hawaiian kid outweighed Freeman's one-hundred and seventy-six pound frame by at least fifty pounds, so he wasn't about to go at him head-on. Freeman never went at anybody head-on unless he was certain of the outcome, and Benny Taupua was built like a walking shoe box.

Freeman told him, "Okay, you got a deal."

"That's day after tomorrow," Benny Taupua said. "Don't make me come looking for you."

He'd moved away then, a set of loose shoulders and tight ass moving through the small crowd of onlookers that parted for him like the Red Sea. Freeman had gone on his way, aware of but unaffected by the snide comments and sneers left in his wake.

At five-thirty the next morning a deputy unlocked the gate and two trustees pushed two metal serving carts inside containing hot trays of powdered eggs, limp toast and watered-down farina. The deputy locked the gate back and hollered, "Hot slop for the hogs that want it."

A few scruffy-looking guys in their underwear straggled up to the carts, pulled out a tray and sat down at one of the tables. Most, however, preferring sleep over slop, never budged from their beds.

Freeman had washed his face and hands at the big round basin next to the open showers and worked his way through *two* trays before the deputy and trustees returned for the carts. Before leaving, the trustees set two mops and mop buckets filled with hot soapy water inside the gate, and suddenly everybody was asleep again.

Freeman had given it another ten minutes before rising from his pad and making his way to the mop buckets. The mops were sticking out of the heavy wringers, freshly squeezed and ready to go.

Just the opportunity he'd been waiting for.

Freeman leaned one of the mops against the wall and hefted the mop wringer. It was made out of steel and weighed at least twenty pounds. He rested it on his shoulder and went down the range to the last cell. Because of the overflow of bodies sleeping on the floor there was no point in locking the cell doors that operated by a lever outside the gate.

They were all asleep in there—double bunks on the left, double bunks on the right. Benny Taupua was in the bottom left bunk. On his side, knees drawn to his chest, face pushed lopsided where it rested on one outstretched arm.

Freeman stepped inside, took a good stance next to the Hawaiian kid's bunk, and slammed the heavy wringer against the big kid's exposed back. Benny Taupua's eyes and mouth flew open and he stiffened like he'd been hit by lightning. But he didn't cry out even with three crushed vertebras, not without any wind in his lungs.

Freeman rolled the Hawaiian kid off the bunk and onto the floor and really went to work on him then, taking advantage of the big guy's temporary paralysis. The second and third blows smashed the kid's left ankle bone, and he did scream then, a piercing wail of pain sounding almost too high-pitched to be human that Freeman cut short with an axe chop to the kid's stomach that sent what little wind he had left whooshing out as he faded into unconsciousness. For the hell of it, Freeman took aim and shattered the kid's other ankle, feeling disappointment when he received no reaction from the now comatose Hawaiian.

Freeman dropped the mop wringer and stepped in between Benny Taupua's splayed legs. He grabbed an ankle in each hand and dragged him out of the cell, aware that the Hawaiian's cellmates were now awake and staring at him. Many of the inmates sleeping on the day-room floor were awake too, sitting up craning their necks around as Freeman tugged Benny Taupua to the gate, gave a final squeeze to each ankle and dropped them hard on the concrete. Benny lay there and groaned for several minutes before the deputy came back to see what was going on. A few minutes later the medical technicians showed up and carted the Hawaiian off on a wire stretcher.

And that was all it took. No one objected when Freeman collected his bedroll and moved into Benny Taupua's bunk. No one ratted on him either, and that included the Hawaiian, whom he never saw again. A detective came up and conducted a few halfhearted interviews but gave up after Benny's ex-cellmates swore on Jesus that the guy had fallen off his bunk that was exactly twenty-seven inches off the floor. And that was the end of it.

Later that evening, when Freeman was in his new cell surrounded by his new admirers, he had a visitor. A skinny Cuban with a pocked face and a silver tooth who stopped in the doorway and said he wanted to talk to him. Freeman told him to come in and his cellmates immediately went out to the dayroom to watch TV.

The Cuban sat down on the bunk across from him, lit a cigarette and said his name was Arturo Guterez. He pulled his lips into a silver-toothed grin and said, "You got style, *homes*."

Freeman leaned back on one elbow and gave the Cuban his blank look, waiting for him to get to the point. The kid was about his own age, but the pocked face made him look at least twenty-three. He had a heavy accent and a thin mustache not yet fully matured.

"But you were lucky he's a stand-up dude, man," the Cuban added, "otherwise you lookin' at a sure deuce in the joint."

"Why should that bother you? That's my problem."

The Cuban had raised his hands. "Hey, *homes,* no need to get an attitude. You did what you had to do and now you got these fools buffaloed. But I want to make you a proposition I think will be good for us both."

"What kind of proposition?"

Arturo told him that he belonged to a small inter-racial group that called themselves The Invaders. There were only nine of them right then, mostly guys fresh out of Lake Butler or Raiford who were looking for new adventures, specifically those associated with the cocaine trade or were wanting to get into it. But they didn't take just anybody, Arturo told him, every-one had their field of expertise, so to speak. They had guys who could pick a lock and guys who could peel and burn a safe; they had a chemist who kept the group solvent by cooking up speed and 'ludes for the yuppie tourists over in Miami Beach, and they had a bona fide demolitions expert who was ex-Navy Seal. They were getting their shit together, Arturo told him, right on the verge of doing big things.

"What kind of things?" Freeman asked him.

"The cocoa, *homes,*" the Cuban told him, and rubbed his fingers together. "*Mucho dinero.*"

"*Mucho* risk, too," Freeman said. "Smuggling."

Arturo had flashed his silver tooth. "You got it wrong, *homes.* We don't smuggle noth-*thing.* We *take* from the smugg-*lers.* Not the major players, the small in-dependents moving five or ten keys up to fucking Min-nesota or somewhere. All it takes is good information, find out who's the mule, and *ka-boom,* we take him first time he gets off the interstate. You like it?"

Freeman had given it about five seconds before saying, "If it's that good, why do you need me?"

"It's not that we *need* you. I told you, I like your style. You got big balls, *homes*. A small group like us, that goes a long way. Tell me, what did they bust you for?"

Freeman told him. The Cuban asked him if he had a record, Freeman said no.

"No sweat, then," Arturo said. "A suspended sentence, probation at the most. You walk out right from the preliminary. I give you a name and a letter, you go see him, he takes care of you. Give you some money and a place to stay. How about it, *homes?* Want to give it a try?"

Freeman did. He'd never considered getting involved with real dope, having done nothing stronger than a little weed, but it wasn't only the promise of long money that swayed him. Freeman had become a believer in destiny, and he'd never forgotten his childhood ambition of diving into human minds and carefully sorting through all the buried debris in search of whatever it was he was after. And if the subject disagreed and offered stiff resistance, then so much the better; half the fun was getting there. Freeman had even coined a private term for his pet passion—mental voyeurism. He liked that, thought it had a catchy ring. He'd even considered keeping a detailed journal filled with such analogies for Ph.D.'s to ponder, because Freeman believed that he was truly unique in his profession. They would understand that this was his destiny.

Arturo's prediction had proved accurate. Because Freeman was a first offender, the Assistant DA handling his case agreed to a reduced plea of unlawful possession of a weapon. Because of his age—not quite twenty at the time—the judge sentenced him to one year probation and a withheld adjudication. Meaning if Freeman stayed clean for the entire year, the arrest and conviction would technically be erased from all official records as if it never happened. The kindly judge told him to learn a trade. Freeman said he would.

The first thing he did after walking out of Superior Court was take a bus to Alvarado Street. The address that the Cuban had given him turned out to be a dilapidated dance studio that had been converted to a used-book store.

Freeman had found Melton Banks, the name that was on the letter of introduction written by Arturo Guterez, sitting behind a counter cataloging a stack of magazines. He was a black kid about the same age as Freeman, with braided hair down to his shoulders, wearing little square granny glasses that Freeman thought looked ridiculous on such a big head. A body-builder type in a leather vest with rawhide laces. The guy had read the letter twice, slowly going over every penciled word written on both sides of the yellow sheet of paper that had been torn from a legal pad. Then he'd given Freeman the once-over and asked if he had a place to crash.

Freeman, having evolved into something of a loner, never did feel quite comfortable with his new cronies. For that matter, they didn't feel very comfortable around him either. There was something strange about him that they couldn't quite put their finger on. He was part of the group solely out of respect for Arturo, who was taking the rap for an extortion scheme that the entire group had participated in.

Freeman decided he would stick around just long enough to score a decent nest egg for the next part of his journey. Less than two weeks later, the opportunity arrived.

Melton Banks wanted to kidnap a charter boat captain who operated out of The Castaways Marina in Lauderdale. There was quiet talk from those in the know that the captain also hired out his forty-two foot custom-made Hatteras with twin three-hundred horsepower diesels to make occasional coke runs from Cuba. The guy didn't belong to any connected organization that anybody knew of, so it followed that he was contracting out to independents who needed a quick way to get their dope out of Castroland without any risk to themselves. The idea was to make the captain give up their identities, how much, how often and where he was hauling, then move in and help themselves. A nice neat little score.

Except the charter boat captain turned out to be difficult. They had snatched him right off the boat in the dead of night, blindfolded and hustled him off to the back room of the used-book store. Melton Banks tied him to a chair and roughed him up as planned, inflicting a great deal of pain but no permanent injuries. But the captain was tough and kept insisting he made his living conducting deep-sea fishing charters and didn't know what the hell they were talking about—*what* fucking cocaine? Then he started *threatening* them, of all things, straining at the ropes with four guys standing around him and screaming about the politicians and cops he knew and how they were in big fucking trouble. Freeman could see big Melton wavering, wondering if they'd made a mistake and if he was just expending good energy for nothing. It was those pesky sensitivities again...that stubborn armadillo.

Freeman had stepped forward and said, "Here, let me talk to him a little. Get me that tube of Super Glue out of the kitchen drawer, will you? Then leave us alone a few minutes."

Melton Banks had been happy to oblige. He was strong as a bull and had the heart of a badger, but he didn't have the stomach for this.

When they were alone, the charter boat captain, a pudgy guy in his early fifties, glared at Freeman and started mouthing the threats again, calling him an idiot for even thinking they could get away with some shit like this—

Freeman had let him wind down a little, then quietly said, "Do you really think you can threaten destiny?"

The boat captain said, "What?"

"I'm your destiny," Freeman had told him, and savored it every time he thought back on the incident. "This is something that was meant to be and there's nothing either one of us could have done to change it."

"You're a lunatic!"

"That's right," Freeman told him, and showed him the Super Glue. "And I'm gonna show you just how big a lunatic I am in exactly two minutes if you don't tell me what I want to hear. After that I'm gonna seal those lips for good. Then I'm gonna tilt that ugly head back and squeeze a drop at a time in each nostril till you can't suck air anymore. Do you understand what I've just told you? After that, there'll be no more discussion."

There was something about the conversational way he put it that made the captain believe every word he said. In less than thirty seconds he had given Freeman the name of the real estate agent in Hollywood that he was hauling sixty keys a month for and who was paying him fifty thou a trip for delivery right at the back door of his two-room office on the corner of Hibiscus Street. Anything else he wanted to know?

Freeman had said no, that would do it, then moved around behind the man and got him in a good tight headlock, the pressure forcing the captain's jaws together as he twisted violently from side to side, trying to get away from Freeman's hand that stayed right with him, squeezing a heavy bead of glue along the crack of his lips that lived up to its warning and bonded instantly. He switched to the nostrils, holding the head firm and gazing into the brown eyes filled with panic as Freeman let drop after steady drop disappear into the dark hairy openings, the man instinctively drawing a final deep breath before they clogged completely. Freeman thought he knew the instant the guy gave up the ghost, could almost visualize his spirit rising up from his body and being sucked right into the air vent.

It was neat.

Freeman had called the guys back in and told them what the charter boat captain said. They listened with half an ear, swinging their heads in disbelief from Freeman to the lifeless body slumped in the chair.

They dumped the charter boat captain deep in the marsh off the Tiamiami Trail, where the 'gators and scavengers would make short work of it, and the next morning took down the real estate agent as he was unlocking the office. After learning the score, the guy hadn't given them any trouble at all, had led them straight to the basement, where he had eleven keys of high-grade cocaine stashed in the bottom of an old metal filing cabinet that at the time was worth twenty-eight thousand dollars a key. They had left the guy taped and gagged on the basement floor, humiliated and scared but very much alive. Melton Banks,

71

not wanting to hit the Tiamiami Trail again quite so soon, had personally stood guard over the man until Freeman McKee was out of the basement.

That night, surrounded by the rest of The Invaders, Melton Banks handed Freeman an envelope with twenty-thousand dollars in it and told him they were parting company. "You're a good man," Melton said, "but you don't fit in with the group. Been nice knowing you."

It hadn't bothered Freeman at all, he'd had the same idea. Besides, he was still flying high on the charter boat captain. No question about it; he'd found his calling.

And somewhere out there was his destiny.

CHAPTER SIX

Larry Twiford and Olive Oyl started in on him as soon as he walked into the office late at nine-twenty, getting on his case even before he had poured his first cup of coffee and checked for messages. Thinking they were being real cute.

Larry saying, "There you are. Been up all night installing that unit out at the Marina?"

Olive Oyl saying, "Don't forget to turn in your work order so I can get a bill out, now."

Larry saying, "What did you give him, microwave? Photo cell?"

Olive Oyl saying, "I bet he talked him into a laser. He was counting commission on his fingers."

Both of them knowing he hadn't installed a damn thing because he hadn't signed the log for any equipment.

Cage said, "Go ahead and have your fun, I'll laugh all the way to the bank."

Larry gave him a look. "Then you did sell something?"

"Yep." Cage allowed himself a touch of smugness for their being so smartass with him.

"Well, *what?*" Larry said.

"Oh . . . a laser, I guess. Wouldn't want to disappoint Olive Oil."

She stuck her tongue out at him and turned to her computer.

"What do you mean, you guess?" Larry said. "Either you did or you didn't. And when are you installing it?"

Cage took his coffee to his desk and sat down, taking his time while Larry reared back in his swivel chair and regarded him with growing impatience.

"Man said I could put in anything I wanted," Cage told him. "And I can install it at my convenience. In addition to that, I did some moonlighting for him last night and picked up an extra grand. The man is a merchant's dream."

"I want to hear this," Brenda said, facing him again.

Cage told them about it, giving them a detailed description of Freeman McKee and the stories he had heard from Ben Hollister and John Malone. By the time he'd finished, Brenda was frowning.

"What a horrible little boy."

"Yeah, well, in a way, you'd probably think he hadn't changed much if you saw him today. He's got this set expression like he's totally unaware of what's going on around him. But then you sit and talk to him for thirty seconds, get a real close look at those eyes, and you realize he isn't missing a goddamn thing."

Larry said, "This Hollister paid you a thousand dollars to have dinner with the guy?"

"Five hundred," Cage said. "The other five's a bonus if they don't hear anything from McKee in three days.

Same deal with the system, anything I want to put in." He saw the look on Larry's face and added, "Don't worry, I wouldn't give him a laser."

"What if McKee hassles them again?"

"Then I'm out five hundred bucks and Banes and Twiford is out a new client. I only have the guy's word for it, Larry, but I got no reason to disbelieve him. Anyway, what could I do about it if he does? I recommended they call the police and file charges but they wanted to do it this way."

Larry came up out of the chair. "Well, I wouldn't worry about it," and headed for the curtained doorway at the rear of the room. "But I wouldn't hold my breath waiting for that extra five hundred and a sale. Day after tomorrow he'll be having a change of heart. If I were you I'd cash that check real quick."

Larry pushed through the curtain as Brenda dug through the clutter of papers on her desk, found the paper she was looking for, got up and brought it to Cage. "Paul called from Hawaii this morning. He wants you to do a parts inventory for our sales rep in St. Louis. He also said to make sure you order three mercury switches, the FY Fives he told you about."

Paul Banes was constantly tinkering in his workshop beyond the curtained doorway that had grown to resemble something out of a CIA movie. Paul built his own systems from scratch and subsequently kept in stock practically every piece of electrical circuitry known to man, at least so it appeared to Cage. Larry said that some of his equipment was even better than the Bureau had when he was with the FBI, and there was literally nothing associated with residential and commercial security systems that Paul Banes didn't know about.

Cage said, "How soon do you have to have it?"

"As long as I can FAX it by Friday," she said, and

went back to her desk to answer the ringing phone.

Larry came back wiping his hands on a wad of toilet paper, telling Brenda there weren't any paper towels in the bathroom, then went "oops," when he saw her on the phone. She listened intently for a moment, then abruptly covered the receiver with one hand and gave Cage a concerned look.

"Allen, you'd better pick up on line two. It's Ben Hollister, and he's babbling, saying you have to get there right away."

Cage picked up the extension. "Ben? What's happening?" He listened, disbelief spreading through his stomach. He didn't waste time asking questions. "I'll be there quick as I can," and hung up.

Larry and Brenda were watching him. "That was Ben Hollister," he said quietly. As if they didn't already know that. "John Malone, his partner I was telling you about. He's dead. Found him in his car in the garage about ten minutes ago. The police are on the way." He paused, gazing off through the big picture window facing Santa Monica Boulevard. "I got to get out there," he said, and swiveled out of his chair.

Larry tossed the wad of toilet paper into his waste basket. "I'll go with you," he said, but Cage was already out the door.

They stepped off the elevator onto the eighteenth floor and were met by a uniformed LAPD officer who had been told to bring Cage straight inside as soon as he got there. The policeman gave Larry the once over and asked who he was. Larry gave him a business card and told him he was ex-FBI, retired, and that Cage was his employee.

"Can't help that," the policeman said, "nobody mentioned anything about you." Relishing the opportunity to put an uppity Fed in his place. "You'll have to wait down in the lobby."

"No problem," Larry said, and stepped back inside the elevator. He wasn't offended. It went like that sometimes.

Ben Hollister, dressed for the tennis court, was hunched over on the couch, staring at his Nikes. He looked up as Cage entered and started to say something, but then closed his mouth and turned away as he seemed to be hit with a sudden chill.

A large man in a wrinkled brown sports coat got up from the love seat and held out his hand. "Allen Cage? My name's Lynn Evers, I'm a sergeant with LAPD Homicide. You mind having a seat?"

Cage sank down at the opposite end of the couch and looked at Ben Hollister. "What the hell happened?"

"A waking nightmare, that's what happened." Ben's voice was tight with fear, he kept licking his lips. "John left a little after seven this morning to take his monkey for a booster shot. A couple hours later I'm leaving to keep a tennis date. I go down to the garage for my car and see John's black Saab still parked next to my Mercedes. I look in the window and—"

He stopped in midsentence and his eyes appeared to lose focus. Cage waited for him to finish, but Ben didn't say anything else.

"Mr. Malone was in the driver's seat," the detective said. "Shot once in the back of the head with a small-caliber handgun. Pretty clean and professional to that point. But the monkey was a different matter. It's head had been cut completely off and stuck on the gear shift. Takes a special kind of deviate to do a thing like that. Don't you agree?"

"I agree."

Ben said, "I got to go to the bathroom," and hurried

from the room holding his stomach.

The detective was in his early fifties, with a salt-and-pepper mustache and thick brown hair, a small shaving nick on his chin. Tired eyes that either didn't sleep much or had become disillusioned by what they had seen. He was sizing Cage up. "Mr. Cage, are you some kind of hired gun?"

"Where do you get a notion like that?"

"Mr. Hollister said he paid you to meet this man Freeman McKee last night and that you did talk to him. That right?"

"Correct."

"Are you a licensed private investigator?"

"I sell security systems, Detective Evers, and you probably know that. I'm sure Mr. Hollister has already explained my involvement in this."

"Yeah, he told me the story. A case of bad judgment, if you ask me. What did you say to the man? Did you lean on him? Threaten him?"

"Wait a minute, don't even try it," Cage said. "You're not putting this on me. I advised them to call the police but they decided on their own approach. I was polite but firm. No threats, no guns, just a mutual understanding—"

"Apparently there was no meeting of the minds," Evers said. He looked to the ocean view past the open patio doors. "I thought nothing much could surprise me anymore, after nineteen years in the business. Thought I'd seen about everything. But when I leaned in that car and saw that monkey's head on the gear shift . . . It was tilted to one side so it would grin at whoever opened the door. Would the person you talked to last night be capable of doing something like that, Mr. Cage?"

He thought about it, choosing his words carefully,

not wanting to give the detective anything he could throw back at him later.

"Freeman McKee doesn't give you much to work with when it comes to making judgments and forming opinions. Talking to him is like having a conversation with a robot, for all the emotion he shows. Hollister and Malone told me they used to call him stoneface when they were kids."

Evers was persistent. "But what does your gut tell you? I know how Ben Hollister feels, but he's biased. Could this guy be as big a terror as he claims? Just give me your best guess."

"I can give you a maybe," Cage said. "Animals and kids wouldn't like him."

Ben Hollister came back into the room. He'd washed his face and Cage thought he caught a whiff of toothpaste as he sat down and ran a nervous finger across his nose.

"Okay," he said, "what happens now?" Then he was struck with another thought. "Oh, Jesus, his folks. Who's gonna tell them?"

"We'll do that, Mr. Hollister," Lynn Evers said. "Of course you can too, if you want, but we have to make it official before releasing his name to the media."

"The media?" Another thing he hadn't thought about. They'd be waiting for him like vultures, pushing cameras and microphones in his face and asking how he felt about the situation. He had to get away from here.

Detective Evers said, "Mr. Hollister, is there any reason you can think of why this ex-classmate of yours would want to harm you or your friend?"

"I'm telling you Freeman McKee is a psycho," Ben said. "He doesn't think like normal people. After the armadillo thing John and I started pulling away from him. Then we decided to leave Houston after graduation and move here to make *sure* we got away from him. Maybe it's been building on him all this time and he decided to get back, I don't know. What I *do* know is that I'm getting out of this place as quick as I can and I'm not coming back till you get that sonofabitch off the streets."

"That's not a bad idea," the detective said. "Just let me know where you are." He looked at Cage. "I don't suppose he mentioned where he was staying?"

"No."

"Any guesses why he picked Kelbo's for the meet?"

"No."

Detective Evers said, "Well, you're a big help." He drew a tired breath, took a business card from his jacket pocket and reached it to Cage. "Go on, get out of here. I want to see you at Parker Center at two o'clock this afternoon for a full statement. Be there."

Cage was doing a slow burn. "I'm not the perpetrator here, Detective Evers. There's no call to talk to me like one."

"If you're offended at that," Evers said, glancing at his watch, "think how you're gonna feel when I lock you up as a material witness in about thirty seconds if you're still here."

Cage believed him. He stood and looked down at Ben Hollister. "I'm sorry about your friend," he said. He pulled out his wallet and took out the five-hundred-dollar check Hollister had given him the day before and placed it on the coffee table. "Under the circumstances, I don't feel right taking this. If there's anything I can do, call me."

Ben fingered his diamond earring and looked away. "I'm not blaming you, I'm the one asked you to talk to him. Keep the money, you earned it."

"Thanks, anyway," Cage said. "I know the way out."

He was almost to the doorway when Detective Evers said, "Mr. Cage?"

He turned around, aware that the man's voice had taken on a more friendly tone.

"Come in at your convenience," the detective said. Just make it soon. Call first and let us know."

Cage nodded and left.

Larry Twiford was over by the lobby door that led to the security garage, talking to a middle-aged man in a gray jumpsuit with LAPD stenciled across the back. He shook hands with the man as he saw Cage step off the elevator and came forward to meet him.

"Everything squared away?"

"Just on hold," Cage told him. "There's a cop up there who isn't quite sure about me yet. Wants me to call and make an appointment to come in and give a statement.

"What's his name?"

"Lynn Evers."

"Don't know him," Larry said, and fell in step with Cage. "The guy I was just talking to, I know him, though. Name's Bill Donner. We attended a three day surveillance and forensics seminar in D.C. four years ago. He's assigned to the Mobile Crime Unit and says it's a real mess in there."

"Did he see the body?"

"He just finished moving it. The monkey's too."

"That detective said its head had been cut completely off and stuck on the gear shift. That right?"

"Bill said taking it off and tagging it was worse than anything he's ever done. You have to wonder what kind of mind could come up with something that sick."

Cage had no answer for that and kept silent as they pushed through the lobby door and out into the circular drive that was filled with official vehicles. Cage paused on the walkway and watched an ambulance just pulling away. The emergency lights were on, there was no need for the siren.

"I was sitting right across from him, Larry," Cage said. "I ate with him, cracked a joke or two. Not for one goddamn minute did I really take him seriously. And all the time he was sitting there playing with me, knowing exactly what he was gonna do. What an idiot."

"Yeah," Larry said. "I know the feeling. But unless you're a mind reader, there's no way of telling what's going on inside a guy's head. Look at that Ted Bundy, there's a case in point. How could anybody figure him for a Jack the Ripper? You never know."

"Normally I'd agree with you," Cage said. "But there's one big difference between Ted Bundy and Freeman McKee."

"What's that?"

"I was warned about Freeman McKee."

CHAPTER SEVEN

After leaving Melton Banks and his Invaders, Freeman had bought a two-year-old black Corvette convertible and a pair of wraparound mirror sunglasses and driven from Miami to New York, and the only time he had put the top up was when he ran into a violent thunderstorm outside Atlanta. It had been summer, Freeman's favorite time of year, and he had been in no hurry. He took the scenic route and hugged the coast all the way to Norfolk before swinging inland, staying in good motels and expanding his wardrobe to include two new Armani suits and two pairs of Salvatore Ferragamo dress shoes. The clothes, combined with the natural way that he carried himself, made Freeman appear five years older, which was the effect he'd been seeking. Freeman McKee wanted to grow up fast. His destiny was out there somewhere, he was positive of that. He wanted to find it quickly.

New York was Freeman's kind of town. Everybody was in a hurry just like he was and everybody had a game. Make the right connections and you could be anything you wanted. Freeman had stood in Times Square his first day in the city, the same spot where they lowered that apple every New Year's Eve while Dick Clark counted backwards from ten . . . had stood there at high noon, surrounded and buffeted by the pedestrian lunch-crunch, and felt a supercharged rush of adrenaline go through him.

Maybe he would find it here.

He paid a month in advance for one room in a bed-and-board motel in the Bronx and went searching for the right connections.

Go into any major city in the country, grease the palms of a few taxi drivers and bell captains, frequent the "colorful" watering holes of the local characters, ask the right questions and listen good, and within seventy-two hours you'll have the name of the man who runs things, the man whose favor a young up-and-comer would want to curry in order to establish his credentials.

The Man in the Bronx was a pudgy Italian named Frankie Moreno who owned a small jewelry-repair shop located above an Italian restaurant that was owned by his wife. Everybody knew the jewelry-repair shop was a front for Frankie's fencing operation, just like they knew the restaurant was a front for Frankie's bookmaking operation. But Frankie paid large juice to the right people, and neither venture caught any heat from the cops. In the Bronx, if you had decent hot jewelry to unload, or if you wanted to place a sporting bet on your favorite team, you had to go through Frankie Moreno.

Freeman had entered the restaurant while The Man was having his dinner one evening with "Dumbo" Pugliesi, his elephantine driver and bodyguard. Free-man walked right up to the table and asked The Man if he could talk to him in private for just a couple minutes about a proposition that would be extremely beneficial to both.

The Man had looked up from his plate of spaghetti, face registering cautious interest, while Dumbo's hands slipped from sight beneath the table.

Frankie liked the no-nonsense, no-ass-kissing way Freeman had approached him while still maintaining proper respect.

"Sit down, kid," Frankie told him, nodding to a chair. "What's on your mind. Don't worry about Dumbo, he hears what I want him to hear."

Freeman had rehearsed his lines, wanting to say it just right so The Man would know he wasn't a ringer or anything. Frankie Moreno looked like a man who recognized potential.

He said: "Mr. Moreno, I just got into town from Houston by way of Miami and I'm looking for someone who might be in need of my particular specialization."

Frankie said, "What specialization is that?"

"Information and eradication," Freeman said, letting it roll off his tongue like he'd been doing it for years, really wanting to impress The Man. "Your own private intelligence officer and disposal system. You think somebody's doing you wrong but can't prove it, give me the nod and I'll guarantee a full confession, if he's guilty, and complete disposal of the subject afterwards." Freeman paused for a short breath and continued. "And just to demonstrate my good faith, I'm going to give you the first one for free. A successful man like yourself must have a few question marks about certain people. Write a name and address and what you want to know on a piece of paper, let me peek at it, then burn it. I'll take it from there. No worries about a wire or a setup, you won't have to say a word. I'd be honored if you'll allow me to do you this service."

To Freeman it was a scene straight out of *The God-father*, the feared Luca Brasi vowing to destroy all enemies of Don Corleone. He even said it the way he thought Luca would say it, even down to the detail of trying to mimic the Italian accent, which was not easy for a Texas boy.

Freeman had expected The Man to go for his offer, so he was unprepared when Frankie Moreno gave him a long, long look, then threw back his head and laughed so hard Freeman could see the fillings in his back teeth, big sow-eared Dumbo the bodyguard joining in, a hunk of garlic bread hanging out of his mouth.

He had sat there and waited for them to finish, feeling a warmth in his gut as he became aware of other customers stretching their necks to view his humiliation. Freeman had remained stoic through it all, choosing the Miller Lite clock behind the small bar to focus on until the outburst was over, then inquired what he had said that was funny.

Frankie had rubbed his eyes and said, "You're priceless, kid. You should've been an actor. Who sent you here, that fuckin' Nicky Barnes over in Harlem? That spade's got one great sense of humor."

"I don't know Nicky Barnes," Freeman told him. "Did you think this was a joke?"

"Either that or you're the biggest fruitcake ever came down the pike. And I got no time or patience for fruitcakes, so carry your ass on outta here, you're spoilin' my dinner."

"*Now*," Dumbo added for emphasis.

Freeman had stood and looked down at them. "I'm not a fruitcake," he said, and left.

*   *   *

Freeman went to the streets and spent fifteen hundred of the four thousand left from the Florida score to buy a .357 Magnum with a six-inch barrel that the black bartender at the strip joint in Bed-Sty had described as being "experienced, but not in the state of New York."

He had then followed The Man for five straight days. He would have followed him for five straight months if necessary. Big Dumbo behind the wheel of the white Lincoln Town Car, Frankie Moreno lounging against the passenger door with his arm flung across the seat-back, surveying his kingdom. Neither having a clue that they were being stalked by a black Corvette with the top up that was merely part of the heavy traffic.

Freeman followed them all the way from West-chester Square, to Hunts Point, to Eastchester and back again, The Man making more stops than a city bus at all points in between. Waving at people on street corners like he was blessing them, having Dumbo wait in a red zone while he hurried into some bar or shop for five or ten minutes, checking on the two guys who operated his jewelry-repair shop on West Farms Square.

The Man felt very safe in his kingdom.

Freeman discovered that each day was bound by two common denominators: Frankie Moreno never left the boundaries of the Bronx, and by five-thirty he was on the way home to his four-bedroom brick house on Gun Hill Road in Eastchester, where his wife's blue Caddy would usually be parked in the driveway. Dumbo would drop him off, then double back on Pelham Parkway to Williamsbridge Road, where he lived alone in a second-floor apartment of a twelve-unit brownstone. Dumbo would pick The Man up again at ten the following morning, and the routine, with minor exceptions, would start all over again.

With Freeman tagging along behind in his black Corvette and mirror wraparound sunglasses, waiting like a patient spider.

On the fifth day he figured he knew enough to make his move. He bought matching brown pants, shirt and cap from a uniform-supply company, a clipboard, some ruled paper and a large padded manila envelope from Thrifty's.

At five-fifteen in the evening, Freeman parked the Corvette on a quiet street around the corner from Frankie Moreno's house, collected his clipboard and manila envelope that now held the Magnum, strolled up The Man's driveway past the blue Caddy and rang the doorbell.

Myra Moreno had given him a cursory inspection through the peephole, saw the uniform and package, and opened the door. She was a silver-blond woman in her early or late thirties, depending on the depth of her makeup, with a pretty face and chubby body. Freeman told her he had a package for Myra Moreno and handed her the clipboard, easing into the doorway while her smile turned into a frown as she held the pen poised above the blank notebook paper.

"Where do I sign?" she had asked.

Freeman reached into the padded envelope and came out with the .357, crowding her backward while he stepped inside and closed the door. The makeup had not been heavy enough to hide the fear creases in her face, and Freeman recomputed her age to be on the plus side of forty.

He forced her to lead him through the house to make sure no one else was there, Freeman slipping on the disposable surgical gloves while he followed her from room to room, listening to her asking what he wanted to hear ... to please not hurt her ... He took her into the bedroom, tied her spreadeagled to the big four-poster brass bed with baling twine, stuck a two-inch wide strip of adhesive tape over her mouth, pulled up a padded chair and waited.

Frankie Moreno showed up forty-five minutes later. Freeman had watched from the upstairs window as The Man stepped out of the Lincoln with a wrapped bundle of fresh laundry under his arm, waved good-bye to Dumbo and unlocked the front door. By now The Man's wife was having difficulty breathing through just her nose, and her terror at suffocating had left a urine stain the size of a softball on the back of her green skirt that had hiked up to her thighs during her struggles.

Frankie went through the house calling Myra's name, sounding impatient as he came up the stairs and entered the bedroom. He stopped short when he saw his wife and dropped the bundle of laundry, reaching under his armpit for the .38 Bulldog ... then froze when Freeman stepped in behind him and placed the barrel of the Magnum against his head.

Freeman said, "I'll take that, Frankie," and lifted the Bulldog from The Man's holster. Then he had let him turn around to get a good eyeful. It took a few moments before it dawned on The Man who he was, and then it had seemed to piss him off more than frighten him.

"You crazy shit," The Man said. "You got any idea what the fuck you're doin'?"

Freeman was beginning to believe no one was afraid of guns anymore. Here was another one who liked to bluster and threaten, thinking he could influence destiny. Freeman couldn't believe his good fortune.

He made Frankie lie face down on the carpet while

he looped the baling twine from The Man's wrists to his ankles and back up around his neck, pulling the slipknots taut until he was bowed backward like a rocking chair.

Freeman remembered standing there looking down at The Man, trussed up like a hog ready for slaughter, and then to Myra Moreno still twisting around on the bed, strange sounds coming from behind her taped lips. He recorded the scene in his mind for posterity. This was control . . . this was *power*. These two human beings now belonged to him. He could do anything he wanted.

He wondered if The Man had any money in the house. He asked him.

"You idiot," Frankie told him. "That what this is all about? Money? I don't keep any fuckin' money here. This look like a bank to you?"

Freeman had seen the wife's eyes switch sharply to Frankie, and knew he was on to something. He ripped the tape from her lips and asked her the same question.

"Underneath the bar in the den," she had said, blurting it out in a shaky voice. Her heavy eyeshadow had smudged so badly it made her look like a raccoon. "There's a latch under the bottom right-hand side that lets it swing out. Oh, God, just take what you want and go."

Frankie had screamed at her, calling her a stupid cunt, and his wife had screamed back, saying Frankie cared more about his fucking money than he did her. Freeman had let them go at it for more than a minute, listening to each blame the other for their predicament, and thought, ain't love grand. Neither of them understanding that fate had brought them all together at this particular point in time and there was nothing any of them could have done to change that, not one thing. Then he had stuck tape over both their mouths and went downstairs to the den.

The latch was spring-loaded and recessed into the wood behind the padded footrail, and it took Freeman a few moments to find it even knowing where to look. He thumbed it back, heard something go *click*, and the bar swung slowly away on hidden hinges to reveal a deep cavity in the floor. Inside the hole was a green metal ammunition box bearing black stencil markings that read: AR–180, .223 cal.

Inside the box, in pressure-banded stacks of hundred-dollar bills, The Man had stashed six-hundred-ten-thousand dollars. Freeman had struck the mother lode.

He found a Hefty trash bag in the kitchen, dumped the money inside and carried it upstairs, where he discovered Myra Moreno lying motionless with eyes bulging and face a mottled purple. She had apparently strangled on her own vomit. Freeman had felt cheated. The situation had given him a charge that needed release, and he had been planning on having some fun with the cow and make Frankie watch. Teach him a lesson for being disrespectful when all Freeman had done was make The Man a good-faith offer of his services. Calling him fruitcake ... crazy ... idiot ...

Frankie had watched his wife choke to death and had panicked. His eyes were rolled back in their sockets and he was flopping around on his belly like a fish out of water, trying to ease the tension on the twine looped around his neck.

Freeman had walked over and put his foot on the back of The Man's neck and brought him back to the present. His eyes fluttered, then settled on Freeman, looking at him upside down.

Freeman said, "Your old lady's dead, Frankie. In a

minute you'll be catching up with her. This is just a little taste of the specialty I was telling you about. I'd really like to give you the full treatment, but I don't have time. Besides, there's nothing else I need to know from you anyway." He'd grabbed a handful of The Man's hair then and leaned down to within a couple inches of his sweaty face. "But if there was, Frankie, you'd *leap* at the chance to tell me. You know why? Because I got ways of getting at the truth faster than sodium pentothal, Frankie. I could make you tell me your dreams if I thought they were interesting enough."

The Man had been ready to pass out on him, almost beyond the point of comprehension, and Freeman didn't want that. "I'm going to kill you now, Frankie," he had said. "It was meant to be." He'd gradually increased the pressure on the back of The Man's neck, hanging onto the twine to steady himself as Frankie Moreno began bucking and thrashing and making liquid sounds in his throat. "Let me know if you feel this," Freeman said, and shifted all his weight to Frankie's neck and gave a quick bounce. There was a faint *crack* like the sound of a snapping twig as Frankie's neck gave way and nearly caused Freeman to lose his balance. He stood there and watched until Frankie quit twitching, then picked up the Hefty bag and left the house, feeling big as a mountain and with one stop left to make.

He had driven straight to the apartment building on Williams Bridge Road and once again parked around the corner. He took his time going up the stairs to the second floor and down the short hallway to Number Nine, knowing this would be what they called an anticlimax compared to Frankie, but still riding high on adrenaline. He took out the Magnum, placed the-barrel against the peephole in the door and rang the bell.

After a moment he heard Dumbo's voice say, "Who is it?"

"Sergeant Destiny, NYPD," Freeman said. "I need to ask you some questions."

Dumbo said, "Sergeant who?"

"Destiny," Freeman repeated. "I'm holding my badge and ID up so you can see it."

"Well, back up a little bit," Dumbo said, "I can't see the—"

Freeman pulled the trigger and the sound of the explosion was deafening in the small hallway. But it had been muffled by the sound of Freeman's heartbeat that pounded in his ears and throbbed at his temples as he felt the Magnum's kick and smelled the pungent odor of cordite before he remembered to hold his breath. Then he had let the Magnum fall to the floor and walked away without examining his handiwork, knowing it wasn't necessary. He had peeled off the surgical gloves on his way back down and dropped them under the stairwell, hearing confused voices and hurrying footsteps from above as he pushed through the fire exit and followed the shadows around the corner to his Corvette. The urge had hit him strong then, and he knew that he had to find a woman soon. While the rush of the evening was still fresh in his mind and his senses at a fever pitch.

Frankie Moreno had called him a fruitcake. Said he was crazy. Talked to him like he was a piece of whale shit on the bottom of the ocean. But Frankie and his fat wife and big Dumbo the fucking elephant would be riding to the morgue while Freeman was riding out of town with six-hundred-ten-thousand dollars of Frankie Moreno's mad money.

Who'd that make crazy?

CHAPTER EIGHT

Cage spent the rest of the morning on the telephone making routine follow-up calls to recent and would-be clients, answering questions and explaining procedures relative to their particular system. Paul Banes called it "dummy-proofing," making certain the customer was thoroughly familiarized with the product and thus eliminating costly false alarms that the client always swore was a malfunction. Then Paul would have to spend valuable man-hours personally checking each circuit to make absolutely certain everything was in perfect working order. Even though Paul carefully tested each component himself before certifying a system as operational. And when Paul Banes said something worked—it worked.

After a quick lunch of a burger and fries at Hamburger Hamlet, Cage went back to the office and started in on Paul's inventory list, wishing that Olive Oyl could break away from her desk long enough to come back and keep him company for a while.

Long enough to erase the mental image of Freeman McKee, hovering against the backdrop of his eyelids like the afterglow of a flashbulb, refusing to go away regardless of how hard he blinked. He replayed the entire meeting over and over again in his mind, reversing and fast-forwarding to selective parts of the conversation, searching his memory for the one thing he might have said or done that could have sent the man into this kind of perverse rage. Cage had been candid but respectful, and the nearest thing to a threat he could recall making had been in response to the man asking what he'd do if he told Cage to go get fucked and mind his own business, or words to that effect.

Cage had said, *Let's hope it doesn't come to that.*

Could that have done it? Was Freeman McKee psycho enough to commit this kind of mayhem in response to a statement that he perceived to be a direct threat? Was his ego so twisted that he felt like he needed to make a point or send some warped message saying he wasn't someone to be taken lightly? And if he *was* that crazy, what would he do next? Go after Ben Hollister? Maybe even himself?

This was a new thought to Cage and the possibility caused him to instinctively wheel around from the open metal drawers of neatly coded electrical components he'd been recording on his clipboard when he heard someone enter behind him.

"Little jumpy there, aren't you?" Larry said, and continued on his way into the small kitchenette. He took a Diet Coke from the fridge, popped the top and came strolling back out.

Cage said, "Did you finish up at Twenty-Twenty Video?"

"Two hours ago. Everything on line and tested."

"Good, then you can help me knock the rest of this inventory out."

"I own the joint, kid, you work for me. Besides, I got to be somewhere at two o'clock."

"Where?"

"Superior Court, Room 108. Remember? I told you last week, I got tagged for jury duty. That big cocaine bust in Englewood last year. They're picking the jury today. I don't even know why they're making me waste my time going down there, but some smartass clerk said I had to. Can you picture that defense attorney's reaction during voir dire when he finds out I'm retired FBI? I won't be there a hot minute."

Cage said, "That's one thing I won't ever have to worry about, being called for jury duty. One of the perks of being a convicted felon. By the way, I'll be leaving a little early today. I called that detective, Lynn Evers, this morning and told him I'd be in at four to give my statement. Might as well get this over with."

Larry pulled a stool away from the workbench and sat on it. "That's right," he said, "your good friend Freeman McKee. In case you're interested, he's got a sheet."

"Well, I wasn't interested until you brought it up. What did he do, impersonate a mannequin?"

"Carrying a concealed weapon, for one. Dade County, Florida, 1981. Suspended sentence and a withheld adjudication. Technically, that one doesn't count, because he was never violated. But the other one damn sure does."

"You make it sound serious."

"Kidnap and murder. That serious enough?"

Cage stopped writing and looked at him, waiting.

"Eight months ago." Larry said, "Phoenix, Arizona.

A coin dealer. Took him from his home to his place of business and made him open the safe. Nobody knows how much he walked off with, but it was probably a bunch. He killed the owner. Left him bound and gagged behind the counter with his neck broken."

"Then how come he's still on the streets?"

"Some hotshot lawyer got him off. They had a positive ID on him from two transients getting ready to sack out in the alley behind the store and saw him come out. They were huddled under a bunch of newspapers or something and he didn't see them. A week later he's trying to unload a rare gold piece at a coin convention in Vegas, not realizing he was peddling what was probably the hottest coin in the whole country at the time. Only about a dozen of them in existence, all registered. Every coin dealer in America was on the lookout for that piece. So they get him in Vegas and ship him back to Phoenix, where the two transients ID him in a lineup. All nice and tidy, right? Open and shut case."

"Not necessarily," Cage said, and opened another drawer. "I learned a long time ago there's no such thing as guilt or innocence—only good and bad arguments."

Larry pursed his lips and waited a beat, then said, "I'll debate that one with you sometime, but in this case you're right. During trial, he testified that he *bought* the fucking piece from the *transients*. His lawyer dug up an old petty larceny warrant that was still outstanding on one, and found out the other was a three-time bigamist who also owed six years' worth of back child support. It was enough to plant a strong seed of reasonable doubt in the minds of the jury, and they came back with a not guilty. He walked free as a bird and nobody's seen him since. Until now."

Cage said, "Well, you win a few and you lose a few.

How'd you learn all this anyway?"

"Jerry Culpepper. Remember him?"

"Yeah. One of your old FBI buddies working out of the L.A. field office."

"Special Agent in Charge. He called here a little earlier and asked Olive Oil where I could be reached. Then he called me over at Twenty-Twenty and spent ten minutes grilling me about your connection with Freeman McKee."

Cage gave him a sharp look. "Why? And how come the FBI's so interested in him?"

Larry squirmed around on the stool, trying to get comfortable and taking note of Cage's growing irritability.

"Now, don't go getting all bent out of shape and think you're being picked on 'cause you're an ex-con. He got a report on what went down out at the Marina this morning and recognized your name. The Bureau started building a profile on McKee as a possible serial killer and issued a Notify-If-Located bulletin to every law enforcement agency in the country. This was right after he walked on the coin dealer killing. Jerry just wanted to know the extent of your involvement, that's all. I told him it went down just the way it read, and he was satisfied."

That mollified Cage a little and he turned back to his work. "What makes them think he might be a serial killer?"

"The M.O. he used in Phoenix, the way he had the guy tied with baling twine in such a way as to bend the head backward at a severe angle. Then his neck was broken, probably by the guy stomping on it or something. That identical technique was used almost ten years ago in another killing in the Bronx, even down to a real close similarity in the knots. Could have been coincidence, but the Bureau doesn't think so. Neither do I. But there wasn't enough probable cause for a warrant."

Cage opened another drawer. "Well, there damn sure is now."

"They already have one signed and sealed, it just needs delivering. And that's why Jerry cleared the air with me. Everything's fine, I just wanted you to know in case they need to talk to you."

"I appreciate it."

Larry eased off the stool and shoved it back under the workbench. "No need for that. It's not like you were a suspect. Just didn't want you getting hit out of the blue with it and flying off the handle."

"Larry, can I ask you something?"

"Sure."

"Why is it everybody around here always seems to be so concerned with my temperament? Do I foam at the mouth, or what?"

Larry passed behind him and gave him a tap on the back of the head on his way to the curtained doorway.

"If I have to answer that," he said, "you're not as bright as a lot of people have given you credit for. See you in the morning."

Then he was through the curtain and gone, leaving Cage alone to ponder the knowledge that he'd agreed to have dinner with a suspected serial killer. One of his major goals in life.

He finished the inventory shortly after three and dropped it on Brenda's desk on the way out the door, saying he was going downtown to give his statement, in case anybody needed to know.

He decided against the Freeway and took Wilshire all the way downtown, arriving at Parker Center with ten minutes to spare. He rode the elevator up to the third floor and followed the arrows to Room 338, Homicide Division, and asked for Det. Lynn Evers.

A bored-looking guy wearing a short-sleeved white shirt and a shoulder holster lifted his eyes from his computer screen and said, "Who wants to know?"

"Allen Cage. I have a four o'clock appointment."

The detective pointed to a closed door across the room. "Go right on in that room over there, close the door and have a seat. I'll let him know you're here."

It was like every other interview room in every police station he'd ever been in; a windowless cube containing a scarred desk, an ashtray, four metal folding chairs, and a waste basket half-filled with styrofoam cups and aluminum soda cans, all of them crushed. Cops and robbers always crushed their cups and cans. A small venting of what was going on inside them.

Cage sat on one of the folding chairs and drummed his fingers on the desk for about three minutes until Det. Lynn Evers came in carrying a yellow legal pad and a brown manila envelope. He dropped them on the desk and nodded to Cage.

"Thanks for being on time," he said. "I'll get you out of here quick as I can. You want a Coke or something? Maybe some coffee?"

"I'll take a Seven-Up, if you got any."

"The machine does," Detective Evers said, and when Cage started digging in his pocket, added, "Forget it, my treat. We got a witness slush fund takes care of that. Be right back."

Evers returned in less than a minute, holding a can of Seven-Up and a Dr. Pepper. He placed the Seven-Up in front of Cage and took a seat across the desk from him. The *pop* and *hiss* of soda cans being opened sounded abnormally loud in the close confinement. Evers drank deeply from his Dr. Pepper, placed the can on the desk. Then he took a ballpoint pen from his shirt pocket and adjusted the legal pad for writing.

"Now, then," he said, "why don't you give it to me from the beginning. Start with how you first came into contact with Ben Hollister and John Malone and go from there."

Cage started with the phone call from Ben Hollister and went straight through without interruption until he got to the part where he was having dinner with Freeman McKee. The detective was using some kind of weird shorthand to keep up with his every word, filling the pages with loops and slants and dotted lines that appeared to be random scribblings.

Lynn Evers said, "Did he give you any indication where he might've come from? Where he lives? What he does?"

"No. I asked him what line of work he was in, he didn't say. I don't think he gave a direct answer to any question. Not that I asked that many."

"I don't suppose you saw his car either?"

"I don't even know if he was driving one. He could've shown up in a taxi."

Evers took a swig of Dr. Pepper and consulted his notes. "Well, I see nothing's changed since this morning. I thought something might've come back to you but you're still no damn help."

"That's all I know. The only time he even gave a hint about himself was saying he'd just come to town on business for a few days and decided to look up his old schoolmates. That, and the fact he dresses good and wears expensive jewelry."

Evers studied his scribbling a while longer, then set the legal pad aside and stretched. "Mr. Cage, I know about your record."

"I never doubted you would."

"I also know you're not a real criminal, not in the literal sense, anyway, so that doesn't influence me one way or the other. I also liked what I saw this morning when you gave that check back to Ben Hollister."

"But you still think I was wrong," Cage said. "Right?"

"Yeah, I think you were wrong. For the simple reason that you *are* an ex-con and technically still on parole, even if it is unconditional. If you and McKee had ended up in some kind of serious hassle last night you couldn't have won any way it went. And I *hope* you didn't have a gun on you."

"I didn't," Cage said, and thought about the little .25 automatic taped behind the nightstand on his side of the bed. He'd bought it at a Pasadena swap meet over a year ago for self-defense and felt better just knowing it was there. If he ever had to use it, he'd be on his way back to federal prison, self-defense or not. But he was a firm believer in the philosophy that it was better to be tried by twelve than carried by six. Evers was right, though, and Cage told him so.

"Then why put yourself in that position?"

"That's easy, I needed the money. How did I know the guy was a suspected serial killer?"

"Where'd you hear that?"

"I've got sources too," Cage said, and mentally kicked himself for the slip. "Did you think it was a big secret?"

"Until he's arrested, you're damn right I did." He turned his head to the wall and said with disgust, "Jesus, I don't believe this," then gulped the rest of his Dr. Pepper, crushed the can and tossed it into the waste basket.

Cage smiled. He couldn't help it.

"Think it's funny? Well, I suggest you tell whoever's giving you this confidential information they'd better put a stop to it. Freeman McKee is nobody to laugh at."

"I couldn't agree more," Cage said. "I was thinking about something else."

Evers waited a moment, then turned his attention to the legal pad. "While you're busy thinking, anything else you can add to this?"

"I've told you everything I know."

Evers nodded and opened the manila envelope. He shook out five mugshots that had been trimmed around the edges to eliminate any reference to the subject's name and place of arrest. He turned them face around toward Cage and aligned them in a neat row.

"Just for the record, do you recognize any of those men?"

Without hesitation Cage tapped the second from the right with his index finger. "This one."

"Who is he?"

"Freeman McKee. The guy I had dinner with last night."

Evers turned the photo over and handed Cage a ballpoint pen. "Sign your name and today's date on the back."

Cage signed and handed the pen back to Evers. The detective gathered up the mugshots and legal pad, scooted the chair back and stood.

"I'll have your statement typed and ready to sign in about twenty minutes. Can you stick around that long?"

"Sure," he said, and checked his watch. Four-thirty-five. Caprita got off at four. She would have left Wilshire Memorial by now, probably be home if she didn't stop at Ralph's first. "Got a phone I can use?"

"Down the corridor to your left. Come back here when you're finished."

Cage had to wait for the phone while a tall black woman with red hair tried to explain to somebody on the other end of the line that she didn't *know* how the fucking Mercedes got stolen. She'd left it in the May Company garage with the windows and doors locked and the stereo in her purse, and when she came back an hour later it was just fucking *gone,* what more could she tell him. She listened a moment, then said, "Oh, kiss my *ass,* I'll get my own ride home," slammed the phone on the hook and stormed away, nearly bowling over a uniformed officer escorting a hand-cuffed prisoner down the corridor. The woman started screaming at the prisoner, a short Latino with a spider web tattooed around his neck. The Latino kicked at her and the uniformed officer tried to get in between them. In a matter of seconds the corridor was filled with police, all converging on the three bodies that were now rolling around in a tangled heap on the beige linoleum. They managed to separate everybody and three detectives hustled the woman away in handcuffs, still screaming that she wanted her Mercedes back.

Just another typical day in your typical big town police station. Cage couldn't wait to get out of there.

He called home and got Caprita's voice on the answering machine on the fourth ring. He waited for the beep, then told her where he was and said he'd be home about five-thirty, he'd explain it to her then. He said he was in a mood to barbecue a couple of steaks with his special sauce she liked so much. He'd stop at West Coast Meats on the way and have them lop off a couple of filets about two inches thick, then swing by J's Market and grab some sweet corn on the cob. How'd that sound? He said he loved her and hung up, then went back to Homicide and shut himself inside the little interview room again. He tilted the folding chair back on two legs and closed his eyes, rocking gently, trying to clear his mind of everything except steaks on the grill and corn on the cob, French bread and salad on the side.

But that hovering image of Freeman McKee refused to go away.

CHAPTER NINE

Freeman McKee moved down Aisle Seven and hesitated at the dry cereal section, debating over Raisin Bran versus Coco Puffs. He decided on Frosted Flakes instead and went on, easing his cart to the side so a young mother with a kid in the basket and nothing else could pass.

He turned the corner and stopped again at the dairy section, selecting a quart of low fat milk, then headed down Aisle Five. Moving slowly, lingering at the coffee section before moving on again, down to the end and around to the vegetable department.

Keeping an eye on Caprita Arciaga, making sure she didn't get lost in the growing crowd at Ralph's. She was making it easy for him in that white uniform. Looked good in it, too. Except he wasn't crazy over the white hose and lace-up flats that didn't do justice to her legs.

They would have to come off.

He strolled off down another aisle, fifty feet and a

dozen shoppers behind Caprita, his blue eyes focused on her buttocks under the snug skirt as she pushed the basket along, gazing at the shelves. Should be about done, Freeman thought, they were on the last aisle now. And all she had was a chicken, a couple cans of vegetables, a carton of Half and Half and some cheese. Spent thirty minutes in a grocery store to buy that little bit of shit. Making him wait. Trying his patience.

He'd been waiting when she pulled out of the driveway that morning and he'd been waiting when she left Wilshire Memorial not quite an hour ago, and he hadn't felt like waiting in the car anymore while she poked along inside Ralph's. So he followed her inside, got a basket and started tossing things in at random that he had no intention of buying.

Freeman had learned that this was the best part—the planning, the stalking, the anticipation. He enjoyed observing a subject for a while at first, closely scrutinizing every action. Like the little nurse up ahead, frowning at the label on a box of Tide like it was the most important thing in life. Freeman bored in on her, watching her with that feeling people get when seeing a tape of John Kennedy riding past that book depository, smiling and waving at the crowd. Democrat or Republican, everybody always thought the same thing.

If he only knew.

She was getting ready to leave now, heading for the packed checkout counters that would keep her another ten or fifteen minutes.

Freeman relaxed a little, not realizing how tense he'd been, and pushed the basket to one side. He walked to the front and stopped to buy a lottery ticket from the machine just inside the entrance, getting a fix on the little nurse's position in line. There she was, counter Number One, the express lane. Seventh in line, smiling at the woman with the kid in the basket just ahead of her.

Freeman put the Lotto ticket in his pocket and went outside.

If she only knew.

Caprita paid for her groceries, gathered up the two plastic sacks and walked out to the parking lot. Her Volvo was parked in the next to last row, third from the back. She was halfway there when she stopped in her tracks, lifted her face to the cloudless sky and said, "Oh, shit." She'd forgotten Tampax. Her period had taken her by surprise that morning—almost a week early—and she'd been unprepared. Her first day was always a gusher and she didn't know if she had enough to even get through the night.

The hell with it, she thought, and continued on toward her car. She wasn't about to fight that line again. She'd just have to make do until morning.

She didn't give a second thought to the well-dressed man leaning into the open trunk of the car parked two spaces away from her Volvo. As she passed behind him, he turned.

"Excuse me, ma'am, I wonder if you'd be kind enough to help me out."

Oh, Lord, another supermarket pickup artist. "Sorry," she said, "I'm in a hurry."

"It'll only take a second. My wallet fell out of my jacket and slipped down inside this space around the spare tire housing. I can see it, but my hand's too big. Think you could just pluck it out for me? I'd appreciate it."

Caprita paused, feeling guilty that she'd misjudged him, then said "sure." She set her bags on the pavement and looked into the trunk. "Where is it?"

He moved closer to her, pointing at something she couldn't see, giving her a good whiff of his English Leather aftershave. "Right there ... see? Where you lift that little flap to uncover the spare tire?"

She leaned closer. "I can't see any—"

Her legs were out from under her and she went head first into the trunk. She let out a shocked gasp, then a yelp of pain as her head banged against the metal fenderwell, causing her to see stars. In the next instant she heard the solid *thunk* of the trunk closing and was surrounded by darkness. A moment later the driver's-side door opened and closed and the engine came to life.

That brought her back to her senses, and she let out a scream of rage and terror that sounded deafening to her inside the tight trunk space but was barely audible twenty feet away.

She screamed again when she felt the car move, and began beating her fists against the trunk lid, unable to believe that she was being abducted from a crowded parking lot in broad daylight without anyone seeing. The thought sent her arms and legs flailing as she attacked the trunk lid with elbows and knees. It was stifling inside the dark trunk, getting more difficult to breath. She could easily suffocate in here ... Oh, God, what's *happening?*

Freeman was heading for the secondary exit that emptied onto a one-way sidestreet, getting really pissed off at all that racket she was making back there. He'd carried it off real slick, moved so fast nobody had seen a thing. He'd even picked up her groceries, figuring she could snack on cheese and canned veggies if this took longer than he expected it would.

Or maybe he wouldn't give her anything, the way she was carrying on.

Freeman rolled down the window, turned on the radio, found a hard rock song and cranked up the volume as far as it would go. The blast that hit him was almost enough to make him change expression. But it blended right in with those irritating thumps coming from the trunk so he could put up with it for a while. Until he found a good spot to pull over and take other measures to shut her up.

He passed two cars on his way to the exit, the occupants giving him dirty looks as he went by with vintage Def Leppard leaping from the cheap rent-a-car stereo loud enough to shake their windows. He turned right onto the side street and juiced his speed up to the legal thirty-five-mile limit, staying in the right-hand lane and keeping an eye out for police. A few blocks farther on he made another right onto Olympic Boulevard and started looking for an out-of-the-way place to park.

Up ahead on the right was the wooden skeleton of a partially completed four-story office building that appeared deserted. Freeman turned onto the gravel driveway and followed it into the underground garage. He drove all the way to the back, parked next to one of the concrete support columns, and cut the engine. Def Leppard immediately died and he was surrounded by silence. Even the little nurse in the trunk had settled down, probably sensing that something was about to happen. He'd keep her in suspense a few more minutes.

He sat still, letting his eyes adjust to the sudden dimness while he checked out the area. The only sound or movement came from the passing traffic out on Olympic.

He got out of the car and walked back to the trunk.

It was still quiet inside. Shit, what if she had a gun in her purse and was laying there just waiting for him to open that trunk. He was slipping.

He went back to the driver's side, leaned in through the window and came out with the .22 Ruger. Then he leaned in again and pulled the trunk release lever and the lid popped open about two inches.

Freeman cocked the .22 and pointed it at the trunk. "Alright, come on out of there. Leave the purse and keep your hands where I can see 'em."

After a moment the lid opened the rest of the way and Caprita crawled out. The white nurse's uniform was soiled and wrinkled and Freeman could see wet perspiration stains under her armpits. She stood on shaky legs and hugged herself, gawking at him while she labored for breath, face glistening with perspiration offset by wet tendrils of brown hair matted against her forehead.

"Please," she said. "I don't know who you are or what you want, but for God's sake don't put me back in there."

"Little warm, huh?"

"It wouldn't take long for a person to die in there on a day like this."

"Don't give me any ideas, foxy. Now lay down on your stomach."

Caprita hesitated.

"What's wrong? Think you're about to get raped? You keep putting thoughts in my head, don't you? Now get down on your belly and don't make me ask you again."

She lowered herself slowly to the floor and stretched out with her cheek against the concrete. "Please, you're making a terrible mistake—"

"Shut up."

She did while he removed her purse from the trunk

and emptied the contents on the floor. He squatted down and examined each individual item before dropping it back in her bag. Caprita watched, every now and then looking to the far end of the garage in the faint hope that someone—*anyone*—might come in. Aside from the trauma she was experiencing from being kidnapped, there was something about the man's impersonal calm that made her skin crawl. There had to be some mistake here. What could this man possibly want from her other than the obvious?

Freeman tossed her purse inside the trunk and stood there tapping the gun lightly against his leg. He studied her for a moment, then hunkered down beside her again.

"Okay, foxy, we're gonna take a little ride and I don't want any shit out of you. So I'm going to tie your hands behind your back and put you back in the trunk, and if I hear even one thump back here between now and the time we get to where we're going, it's bad news. Hear me?"

Caprita twisted around in a flair of anger. "Don't you understand"—and got a sharp rap to the back of her head with the pistol that sent sparks to her brain.

"*You* don't understand, foxy. You don't have a say in this. Neither one of us does. We got a twenty-minute trip at most, depending on whether or not you're a good girl. You can handle that. Now put your hands behind your back."

Caprita did as she was told, scrunching her face against the pain in her head.

Freeman took a roll of baling twine from his pocket, twisted Caprita's arms behind her back and bound her wrists with the sure moves of an expert—hands turned away from each other so she couldn't tamper with the knots.

Caprita tensed as she felt the hands linger against

her buttocks, then slide downward along the back side of her leg, pausing again at the hem of her skirt that had hiked up to midthigh. She had to distract him somehow, take him away from the mood he was working himself into.

"Listen," she said, "someone had to see us back there. You can't just kidnap somebody in a busy parking lot in the middle of the day and not be noticed."

The hand was creeping beneath her skirt now, moving lightly up the back of her thigh.

"I'm sure the police have your license number right now," she said, her voice with an edge of desperation. "If you'll just let me go before this gets out of hand, I promise I won't say a word to the authorities."

The hand continued moving upward. Caprita squeezed her eyes closed and bit her lip.

"Please," she whispered, "you don't need to do this. It's not too late to—"

"I told you to shut up. You're starting to get on my nerves."

Caprita gave up for the moment, trying to control her rising panic. She couldn't do herself any good by falling apart. This was no longer a question of rape; she'd steeled herself to that. It was now a question of survival.

Both hands were under her skirt now, rolling down her nylon, slipping it off with her shoe and throwing both into the open trunk. He did the same with her other leg, taking his time, rolling the nylon between his palms in what was supposed to be a sensual manner. It felt like two giant slugs creeping down her legs, leaving a slimy trail in their wake.

Freeman settled back on his heels and admired her legs. Lean, smooth and lightly tanned, the way he liked them. Too nice to keep hidden under those puke stockings and crepe-soled shoes.

He turned his head away then and scolded himself for being distracted from his true purpose. Without self-discipline, lust was weakness, a serious chink in a man's armor that could warp his judgment and lessen his resolve. He would control his urge for now. Save it for the proper time when the business at hand was finished.

"Okay, foxy," Freeman said, "on your feet. Time to get back in the trunk."

He stood and saw the look of surprise that came across her face as she started scrambling around to get up. He made no move to help, allowing himself the treat of seeing her white skirt riding high enough to give him a quick flash of white panties so sheer he could see the shadow of her dark pubic hair. She would definitely be worth waiting for. He would have to put a little thought into the occasion. Make it special.

She finally made it upright, tottered to the rear of the car and climbed awkwardly into the trunk . . . toppling into it, actually, giving Freeman a good rear shot as she did a tuck and roll and landed on her hands with a cry of pain. She wiggled around and managed to turn onto her side, lifting her eyes to him.

"Thank you for not hurting me," she said, putting as much sincerity into her voice as she could manage. "I'm sure this whole thing is just one huge misunderstanding and we can get it cleared up right away." She managed a weak smile. "Incidentally, my name's Caprita. What's yours?"

Freeman said, "Oh, that's just beautiful," and slammed the trunk lid in her face. Trying psychology bullshit on *him?*

He went to the glove compartment and took out a Phillips head screwdriver and the two California license plates that had originally come with the Dodge but had been replaced with a pair he'd stolen off a Willys Jeep that afternoon. He switched them back and sent the stolen plates sailing one behind the other across the width of the garage. They struck the far wall with a clanging that echoed through the empty garage. Let foxy hang on to her illusions. He'd use a little psychology of his own.

Almost forgot something. This split-tail was already affecting his judgment.

He leaned close to the trunk. "Hey, what's your phone number?"

She gave it to him, her voice muffled by the lid, then asked why he wanted it.

"I'm gonna call your boyfriend," he said. "See how bad he wants you back."

CHAPTER TEN

Cage got home at six-forty, pulled into the carport and was surprised when he didn't see Caprita's Volvo. She was usually home by five at the latest, even if she stopped by Ralph's on the way. Unless she went to the mall. She could spend hours in that place, zipping in and out of shops, trying on every outfit that caught her fancy. When she was in that mood, time stood still until she browsed her way out of it. Every now and then she'd even buy something.

He collected his packages and entered the apartment from the patio. He had two nice porterhouses with thick filets, a premade salad, two huge ears of sweet corn and a good bottle of red wine, on sale. All he had to do was fire up the grill, whip up a batch of his super secret barbecue sauce, and they could pig out. If Caprita ever got home.

He stuck everything in the refrigerator, then saw Grits the cat come wandering in and go to his food bowl. It was empty. Grits sat down and gave him an indignant look, too cool for words.

"Don't blame me," Cage said, "I don't know where she is. Tell you what, give me a big meow and I'll take care of you."

Grits looked at him.

Cage said, "I don't know why in the hell I keep talking to you. Just like I don't know why you sit there listening to me."

He got the box of Tender Vittles from under the sink and poured a generous portion. Grits sniffed it cautiously, then hunkered down and dug in. When it came to chow, Grits was not a finicky cat.

Cage stripped off his jacket on the way into the bedroom. The blinking red light on the telephone indicated they had messages. He went to the nightstand and pushed the playback button and listened while he undressed.

"Hey, you guys, it's Bev. Just wanted you to know I'm having another one of my little sociables Saturday night and of course you're both invited. And yes, Allen, we *do* have Seven-up. See ya." *Click.*

"Hello, honey, it's your poor mother calling to find out why she hasn't heard from her only daughter in two weeks now. No, it's been closer to *three* weeks. I didn't count the weekend your father and I went out on the boat, which we shouldn't have done because it was overcast and drizzling and all I did was get seasick, and you know I normally *never* get seasick." (Deep sigh) "Anyway, I just called to see if maybe you had time to talk for a few minutes, but I can see you're not there. If you feel like it, you can call me when you get home. It's your father's bowling night and I'll be home all by myself, so, maybe I'll talk to you later. Bye, now." *Click.*

"Yes, Mr. Cage? This is Andrew from Events Unlimited? I have those two tickets you wanted for the Lyle

Lovett concert. He's performing at the Universal Amphitheater a week from Friday, not the Greek Amphitheater like you thought. I got you great seats, close enough to even see his lips move." (Laughter). "Seriously, they're in the best section of the theater, you'll love them. Sooooo, I'll wait for your call. That's 555–7100, extension 322. Take care." *Click.*

"Hey, motherfucker, I got your woman."

Cage went still on the edge of the bed, shirtless, one shoe off, one on, felt his chest go numb. The off shoe slipped from his fingers and fell softly to the carpet as he rose slowly to his feet, gaping at the telephone, experiencing a roaring in his ears swelling into a crescendo that left the rest of the message indistinguishable. After a moment he reached down and pressed the rewind button, noticing that his hand was trembling. He stopped the tape and listened again.

" . . . fucker, I got your woman. And I'm keeping her till you and me square things, so it looks like it's come to that after all. I'm not gonna go through a big song and dance about what to expect if you call the police or tell any other human being alive what's going on and I find out about it. You know. And you know I'll enjoy it. So stick close to the phone after you get this, 'cause I'll be calling you soon and explain how you can get your little foxy back, and I'd better not get an answering machine or a busy signal. And if the line's tapped or somebody tries to run a trace, I'll know it. You're not dealing with an amateur here, clown. You wanted to stick your nose someplace it didn't belong, you pay the price." (Pause). "Have a nice day."

Click.

Cage recognized that colorless voice immediately. And it had a suspected serial killer's dossier to back it up.

Cage turned his head to the console TV, to the eight-by-ten color photo of Caprita that smiled back at him, full of life, adventure.

And motherhood.

"Oh Jesus," he said out loud.

He was dressed and waiting in the living room. Sitting stiff in the easy chair with the lights off and the TV on MUTE. The telephone beside him on the floor. Caprita had once pointed out that he seemed to have an aversion to direct lighting, and he supposed she was right. Up till then he hadn't thought about it, but when he did, he could see what she was getting at. He told her it was a side effect of nearly a year and a half of solitary in Marion, the government's toughest federal prison. In the special unit where he'd been housed, the cells were lit by recessed ceiling lights that burned twenty-four hours a day. He had to blindfold himself before he could even sleep.

Freeman McKee had been outside the window last night. No doubt about that now. Peeking in through the crack in the blinds like the pervert he was, burglarizing their privacy. Would he have her tied up now with that baling twine he'd used on the others, screaming in pain, her body bent back . . .

His imagination got the best of him and he was on his feet. He launched a kick at the glass coffee table and shattered it, sending fragments of glass flying in all directions and Grits scrambling to get behind the couch.

Starting to lose it. He took a ragged breath and forced himself to sit back down.

Cage referred to his inner voice of reason as his own private dinosaur. In times of big trouble or confusion, it came roaring up from the tarpits of his mind, ready to kick mental ass.

It came at him now: *Well, that was real intelligent. You just drop-kicked an eight-hundred-dollar coffee table into oblivion. Don't that make you feel better? Caprita better off?*

He leaned his head back and closed his eyes, willed his heart to slow the tempo. After a while the pounding in his temples ceased and his breathing came easier.

That's better. Now, what are your options?

None. Freeman McKee had eliminated them with his insistence that he stay by the phone; he could call the next minute or the next hour. He didn't dare leave the apartment. Same thing if he got on the phone to tell somebody and McKee decided to pick that time to call. Taps and traces were out. McKee had said he would know if that was happening, and he couldn't gamble that the man was running a bluff. Not if there was the slightest possibility that it could hurt Caprita. With the right equipment McKee could detect an overload on the wire right through the receiver cable— sure sign of additional activity on the line. And he could buy an updated version of Continental Telephone's Private Sentry Device from any phone company in the country that would do just that.

So he would sit here and wait for the call. And he would do whatever Freeman McKee asked him to do. Even if it meant he had—

The telephone rang. He steadied himself and waited for the second ring before he picked up and said hello.

"I sure hope you paid attention to my message and kept this little deal between us," Freeman McKee said. "If you didn't you just killed her."

"I did."

"You did what, killed her?"

"No. Kept it between us. And that's the way it'll stay if you let the woman go." He was astonished to realize he couldn't bring himself to say her name. As if not doing so would somehow make it more impersonal and easier to talk about her.

"I don't think so," Freeman said. "Not yet. Hang on."

The line went silent for about five seconds. Then: "Okay, I believe you. See how trusting I am?"

In a forced normal tone Cage said, "What's this all about, McKee?"

"I just decided that since you like being in my business so much, I'd go ahead and let you take care of the rest of it. Know what I mean?"

"No, I don't know."

"That's okay, we can't all be perceptive. Now listen real good."

Cage, straining his ears for any sound that might help identify the man's location, heard the rustling noise of paper being handled.

"Several years ago Ben Hollister discovered a new substance used for coating computer chips. He called it Duracon-L and took out a patent. I want a computer printout of its exact chemical composition, reduced to standar ... to standardized international equations that will allow instant analysis and identification of the total substance."

The man was reading from something. What the hell?

Cage said, "What's that have to do with us?"

"Your mission, should you decide to accept it, and I believe you will, is to get it for me."

"*Me?*"

"That's right, clown. Convince him, make him see it's in everybody's best interest to cooperate. I don't care what you have to do, just get it. And it better not be some bogus shit you and him dreamed up to throw me off, 'cause the formula's gonna be run through a computer before I turn your girl loose."

So that was the business Freeman McKee had come to town for. "How am I supposed to do that?"

"Tell him what the story is, he got you into this, now get you out."

"If he refuses—?"

"You don't take no for an answer. I'm not going to take it from you. They hired you to persuade me, you ought to be real good at it."

Cage was having trouble maintaining the calm façade. But he had known other Freeman McKees in prison. You couldn't challenge them, make them lose face. That's when they were most dangerous.

Cage said, "All right. What then?"

"You agreed awful quick there, slick. You didn't even wait for me to tell you some of the pleasures I'm gonna have with your girl if you aren't sensible about this."

"I have a pretty good idea," Cage said. "That's why there's nothing to think about. I'll do whatever you say."

"Now there's a revelation. A man with sense. You'd be surprised how few have that anymore. Anyway, what you do then is bring them both to a place I'll tell you about later, and you still don't take no for an answer."

Bring them *both?* Cage said. "Both who?"

"Batman and Robin, clown. Who do you think?"

" ...John Malone's *dead.*"

Silence. Cage held his breath, afraid he might have said the wrong thing, his head so filled with visions of Caprita that it took a few seconds for McKee's reaction to sink in.

"What do you mean dead?" There was a hint of edginess in McKee's tone. "What kind of shit are you trying to pull?"

Play it straight. "He was found in his car in the condo garage, shot in the back of the head. About seven o'clock this morning."

"You're lying."

"Check it out." He waited a beat, confusion adding to fear. This wasn't any act the man was putting on for his benefit. "McKee, you saying you didn't kill him? Because if you didn't then we need to get this straightened out." He waited another beat, considering his moves, then said quietly, "The police think you did it, and up till right now I thought the same thing. But I believe you. Let her go and I give you my word I'll help you prove—"

"Stay there, I have to think about this," and hung up.

Cage slammed the phone into its cradle and turned around on his heel, glass crunching under his shoe. He took three deep breaths, counted to a slow ten before he felt in control again.

He sank into the easy chair and felt his eyes drawn to the soft glow of the fish tank, at the graceful angelfish floating lazily among the artificial seaweed, a school of brightly colored neons darting around the wrecked ship, a pair of puffer fish rising gently to the surface beneath a tiny cloud of bubbles. All calm and serene.

He picked up the telephone and held it to his ear. The dial tone was steady and strong, so he hadn't broken it.

He replaced it softly in the cradle, leaned his head back and closed his eyes.

A few minutes later it rang again. Cage snatched it up.

"McKee?"

"Shut up and listen. Scratch my first instruction. Sit on Ben Hollister and make sure you can get to

him on short notice. I'll call you this same time tomorrow and tell you where to bring him and when,
and I don't want to be hearing any excuses. Same
rules, no cops. Get me Hollister, you get the nurse.
We straight?"

"Very straight," Cage told him. "Look, don't hurt
her, okay? We have a deal. I'll live up to my end. All
I ask is you live up to yours."

Silence.

"Tell her you talked to me, tell her I said it's
gonna be all right, I'll do whatever it takes to get her
back—"

"Cage, you're not gonna threaten me, are you?"

"Jesus, *no*. I'm in no position to do that."

"Well, that's refreshing. Seems a whole lot of people
are doing that nowadays."

CHAPTER ELEVEN

Caprita had never been so terrified, not even on the boat coming back from Nicaragua with that huge red-headed man who was planning to kill them before they got to Ensenada. The difference, of course, was that Allen had been with her, she hadn't been *alone*. Not like now.

And she hadn't been gagged with a two-inch-wide strip of adhesive tape that encircled her head like a turban, restricting her breathing and chafing her skin and creating a maddening itch that she couldn't scratch.

She arched her back and tested the restraints binding her wrists to one of the vertical posts in the headboard of the queen-size bed. He had retied her hands, pulling her arms between the posts and looping the heavy twine tightly around her wrists in a way that suggested he had done this before. It bit into her flesh and made her fingers go numb. Then he had moved to her ankles and done the same, stretching her legs straight out and securing them to the base of the foot-board. Like a lamb to be slaughtered.

She gave up and relaxed a moment with her breasts heaving beneath the wrinkled white blouse. She took in her surroundings again.

She was in some kind of cabin—not rustic, a modern imitation found in theme motels that were supposed to be cozy and intimate. One large main room with a bathroom and partitioned kitchenette with the ceiling light on; cheap replicas of wooden furniture, a hard-wood floor, a phony bearskin rug in front of a fake fire-place; two small windows, one covered with blackout drapes, the other supporting a built-in air conditioner that sounded like it had gravel in it; a TV set on the end of the dresser showing an adult movie, the volume off. The only other items were two plastic potted trees, an ashtray, an unzipped tan suitcase on the baggage rack, and a cassette recorder on the nightstand next to the telephone that might just as well be a thousand miles away for all the good it was doing her.

The man had told her just before he left that the recorder would pick up any sounds she made trying to get someone's attention, if that's what she had in mind. He said that if he came back and heard any noises on the tape that he considered efforts to create attention he would drown her in the toilet. He said it in such a matter of fact way that she believed him. He said the tape would run for an hour and that he would be back by then. How long ago was that? He'd taken her watch, along with her spun gold necklace, her amethyst ring, even her small diamond ear studs. Anything that she could possibly use to free herself.

She wiggled around to get a closer look at the cas-sette recorder. The tape was two-thirds gone, which gave her about another fifteen minutes before he re-turned.

He'd gone to call Allen. It had to be past eight by now and he would be home, worried about her. Would he know what this was all about? The man hadn't given her a hint. They had driven longer than twenty minutes (more like an hour) and by the time he stopped the car and opened the trunk she was suffering from dehydration and heat exhaustion and on the verge of fainting. She had been vaguely aware of being lifted out of the trunk and carried into coolness and soft comfort. He gave her a drink of water and a damp towel and allowed her a few minutes to get herself together. Then he tied her to the bed and left.

Her stretched-out position was putting pressure on her bladder, and she had to go to the bathroom. She was thirsty and felt icky between her legs from the saturated Tampax she hadn't been able to change. She had an extra one in her purse, maybe he would... *forget that.*

She wished that she could turn the TV off. Her eyes kept being drawn to the screen, uncomfortable with the antics that were taking place; a sex scene between a doctor and nurse, the woman on an examination table with her legs splayed and feet resting in the extended metal stirrups. She was fully clothed in a nurse's uniform, but the short skirt was hiked up around her waist to show she wasn't wearing panties. The nude doctor was standing between her legs, fondling his erection with one hand as he stroked the woman's vagina with the other. He wore only a stethoscope around his neck.

She turned away and changed her thoughts. She wondered if Allen had fed Grits, then wondered why she would think of something like that at a time like this.

She heard a key in the door.

She lifted her head and stared at the opening door—

please, let it be a maid. It wasn't. He came in carrying a blue duffle bag and a newspaper and locked the door behind him. He stood there for a moment, looking down at her, then crossed the room to the accordion-door closet and placed the duffle bag on the shelf.

Back turned, he said, "I know what you were thinking when I came in. Hoping it might've been a maid or something, right? Well, don't worry about that. This is a nice little adult motel on the edge of town that specializes in privacy. No maid service, no disturbances. Unless you ask for it. And I didn't ask for it."

He turned to her then, fixing her with those creepy blue eyes that made her think of an owl. "It's just you and me, foxy. No happy storybook ending here."

He turned to the TV, drawing Caprita's eyes to the screen again. The doctor was making love to the nurse now, gripping the woman's hips as he plunged and withdrew.

"Like the entertainment? Your kind of people. It's called *A Turn For The Nurse.* I've seen it before. I get a kick turning the sound off and making up my own dialogue."

He watched a moment longer, then said, "Well, enjoy," and headed for the table by the window. He remembered the cassette recorder and came back for it. He put it on PLAY and placed it on the table, switched on the overhead lamp and sat down. He adjusted the volume on the recorder, unfolded the paper and began to read, dismissing her as if she wasn't even there.

Caprita turned her head away and closed her eyes. She wanted to know if he'd talked to Allen. What did he say? What was he doing? Was he making arrangements to have her freed? Did he understand what this was all about? Jesus Christ, why wouldn't the man *tell* her something?

She really needed to go to the bathroom.

It was right there on page one of the *Evening Outlook,* a Santa Monica paper that was the only afternoon edition he could find. Half-inch headlines spread across the page:

POLICE HUNT DERANGED KILLER

Under that, in smaller caps:

BIZARRE MURDER IN MARINA HI-RISE

He read the account from beginning to end, going slowly, struggling over some of the words because he never did read that well. When he finished he read it again, counting the number of times his name was mentioned: six. Only they were spelling it "McKey," saying he was the "prime suspect" and that the FBI had entered the case because of the "likelihood that McKey has fled the state." It said that the FBI was interested in questioning him about his movements over the last decade "to determine if McKey can be linked to similar crimes in other jurisdictions."

The part about the monkey's head being "decapitated and impaled on the gear shift" offended him. Not that he was bothered by principles, but by the idea that whoever was trying to frame him was making him look bad. Painting him to be some kind of monster. Now, who knew him well enough to believe they could sell such an image to the cops?

Ben Hollister. He was the only one.

He pushed the paper away and slouched in the chair, face tilted upward toward the beamed ceiling, and thought about Ben Hollister. He never did trust that prick, even when they were kids. Something shifty about him. Ben wanted to quit running with him worse than a hog wanted slop, but he never had the guts to come right out and say, "Freeman, I don't want to fuck with you anymore, so get out of my face." Neither did John Malone, for that matter, but Ben was the instigator. Always ready with a quick answer and a wide smile, like a goddam Jack-O-Lantern, while all the time figuring the odds and playing the percentages, looking out for number one. He had enjoyed making him sweat.

Now he was going to make Ben Hollister pay for bum-rapping him and making him out to be a monkey killer. It didn't fit the self-styled image he'd built of himself over the years, which he figured was a cross between Charles Bronson and Charles Manson. He admired the way old Charlie could still inspire fear even after twenty years of maximum security, even when he was an old man and the only way he was ever going to get out was in a pine box. He'd get bored and call "Geraldo" or "Hard Copy," and they'd come running, Charlie sitting on a stool in front of the camera, flapping his arms and acting crazy and saying he was the devil. A few days later the producers and TV stations would get eighty zillion letters from viewers who agreed with him and wanted reassurance that Charlie would die nowhere but in prison. Meanwhile Charlie was getting off on all the attention. He loved it. Shit, what else did he have to do?

Anyway, it was Freeman's opinion that being labeled a monkey killer did not exactly project a favorable impression. For whatever reason, Ben had jumped on the opportunity to get rid of his buddy and pin it on him. Oh, he did it, all right, Freeman didn't question that. It fit right in with the sneaky bastard's disposition. And it had complicated things, made him improvise. Freeman hated to do that.

Caprita was making sounds in her throat, trying to get his attention. He'd been concentrating so hard on Ben Hollister he'd almost forgot about the little nurse.

He raised the volume on the cassette recorder, filling the room with amplified static, got up and walked over to the bed. She looked up at him, eyes holding a silent plea.

"I know," Freeman said, "you got to go to the bathroom, right?"

Caprita nodded.

Freeman let his gaze drop to her skirt. It had twisted high enough around her upper thighs to give him a glimpse of vee-shaped panties, weakening his resolve not to take his pleasure until the business at hand was finished. But he told himself it didn't matter now, he was already having to improvise. He needed a release for the stress that was knotting his stomach and giving him gas ever since the clown told him about John Malone and his monkey. He was confident that, truth be told, there was a private place in the little nurse's heart that would even welcome his attention. All women had hidden desires to have a man dominate them, every one of them whores under the skin. Besides, he knew one of foxy's juicy little secrets.

Freeman took a pen knife from his pants pocket and sat down on the edge of the bed. Caprita flinched when he rolled her head to one side, inserted the blade beneath the adhesive at the nape of her neck and sliced through with one stroke. He peeled away the strips with quick, jerky motions until she was able to draw her first full breath in hours.

"Thank you," she said between gasps. "I have a

deviated septum and it's very difficult breathing through just my nose."

That was a lie, but she was trying to dissuade him from taping her mouth again.

"Dangerous, too," Freeman said. "A person could gag and choke to death on his own vomit."

"Yes, true. I'm sure you don't want to kill me . . . do you?"

Freeman rested his hand on Caprita's bare thigh and began tracing small circles on her skin with his fingers. She looked away, fought against flinching. She knew it would come to this and had tried to prepare herself to deal with it. The thing was to survive.

Freeman said, "Now why would I want to kill a fox like you? That would be a waste." He eased his hand upward, touching her lightly. "Of course, nobody knows what fate may have planned a little farther down the road. It's not really up to us. Tell me, miss foxy—do you believe in fate?" The hand inched higher, sliding beneath her bunched skirt. "If you don't, you're wrong. See, we're all on this earth for a reason, every one of us fulfilling a destiny. A purpose, a mission, a goal—call it what you want, we're here to fulfill it. Just like you and I are here right now. It was meant to be. If it wasn't, it wouldn't have happened. Ever look at it that way?"

She had to look at him then, to see if he was for real. Those icy blue eyes seemed to pull and hold her for a moment before she managed to break contact. Oh, God, what do you say to a madman?

Freeman said, "Yeah, I know you, miss foxy. I know your needs and I'm gonna take care of them. You want a baby real bad, don't you?"

Caprita jerked her head toward him. "You were eavesdropping on us last night, weren't you? That's why Allen went outside, he suspected something.

What's going *on?* You're not taking this kind of crazy risk for ransom or just to get laid. If you'd—"

She broke off in midsentence and bit her lip as she felt the hand pushing between her closed thighs, the fingers making a passage beneath the panties and panty shield. They paused near her vagina, touching her pubic hair.

"I'll make you a baby, foxy. I don't know how long you'll have it. But I'll make you one. And you can enjoy yourself without any hangups about guilt, because like I told you, you don't have any choice. See? Getting wet down there already, aren't we?"

Through clenched teeth, Caprita said, "It's my period, damn you."

Freeman jerked his hand back and stared at his fingers. A vein began pulsing in his right temple.

"I think there's a Tampax in my purse. If you'd get it for me and let—"

He slapped her, a quick backhand blow that caught her high on the cheekbone. He took hold of her hair with one hand and straddled her, rubbing the fingers across her face, hard enough to twist her features as he scrubbed areas already left sensitive from the tape.

"Whore," he said. "Dirty me up. I ought to kill you right now, I ought to twist that skinny neck of yours right around till you kiss the fucking mattress," and to punctuate his words he slapped her again, this time on the other cheek.

Suddenly he pushed off of her and went into the bathroom. She sobbed quietly, face turned to the pillow, while he scoured his hands under the hot water tap for ten minutes, using up nearly an entire minibar of soap.

He came out drying his hands and stood at the foot of the bed, watching her in silence, using the towel like he was scrubbing for surgery. After a moment he went out to the car and came back with her purse. He dumped the contents on the dresser, picked out the Tampax and tossed it on the bed. He came over, pulling out the knife again and flicked it open. He leaned over the footboard and with one quick motion sliced through the twine binding her ankles, then moved around the bed and did the same thing with her wrists.

"Get in the bathroom and clean yourself. Leave the door cracked. You got fifteen minutes."

She almost fell getting out of the bed but caught herself and got into the bathroom.

He popped two Rolaids and began to pace, hoping to settle his stomach juices that were acting up again. Going back to when he was seven, sitting on the potty, curious about the thick pad stained with blood that was half hidden in the wastebasket. Pulling it out, holding it up with two fingers ... his mom coming in, not knowing he was there, in a rage of humiliation, calling him a shameless little beast, wrapping a flabby arm around his neck and smearing the foul-smelling thing across his nostrils and lips.

"Go on, take a good look." She was screeching. "Do you *like* it? How *dare* you embarrass your mother? Go on, *smell* it ... "

She never did like him much after that. She hadn't wanted him to begin with. Whenever she got pissed at him for some imagined wrong she called him a testimonial to God's sense of humor and said that you couldn't even trust a diaphragm anymore. Throwing stuff around, carrying on about how she'd been right there, making it in the pro rodeo circuit until *he* came along ... Well, screw her and his pussy-whipped old man too.

He turned off the TV and sat down at the window table, his eye on the crack in the bathroom door.

He'd make her pay for that.

CHAPTER TWELVE

Larry Twiford came down the stairs belting his gray robe over brown-striped pajamas, wearing a sleepy-evil expression and vowing that whoever was ringing his door bell at 1:20 A.M. better have a damn good reason.

He opened the door and his scowl turned to puzzlement when he saw Cage standing there with his hands jammed into the pockets of his unzipped windbreaker.

Larry said, "Jesus Christ, what are you doing here? You look like the grim reaper."

"Larry, I need to talk to you."

That simple statement, the way he said it, the way he looked standing hunched under the bright porch light as if he were cold, cleared away the last of Larry's sleep fog. He took Cage by the arm. "Get in here."

Larry took him to the kitchen, switched on the light and sat him down at the breakfast table. He was upset by his friend's appearance, at the deep lines and ashen color in his face that made him look five years older.

"I'll make some coffee," Larry said.

"I don't want coffee, I'm not gonna be here that long. Larry, Caprita's been kidnapped. That bastard Freeman McKee took her. He just took her and he's holding her, he's got her somewhere right now doing God only knows what to her, and if I don't talk to somebody besides myself real quick I'm gonna go berserk. So will you sit down and talk to me, Larry? I'm scared to death."

Larry sank into a chair across from him. "*Kidnapped?* What the hell for?"

"Because of me. He said if I wanted to stick my nose in his business I'd have to pay the price, or words to that effect."

"You talked to him?"

"He called me last night. Said if I want her back I have to do something for him."

"What?"

Cage told him the whole story, stumbling over his words in a couple of places, trying to rush it so Larry couldn't interrupt him and waste valuable time asking for explanations. He concluded by stating Freeman's demands for releasing Caprita, then fell silent, directing his thoughts inward until Larry had recovered enough to comment.

"So that's it," he said. "Industrial espionage. Not the normal way of doing it, though."

"McKee isn't your normal industrial spy," Cage said. "You should know that by now. But something doesn't make sense about this, Larry."

"That's an understatement."

"I'm talking about this whole goddamn deal, not just the way he's going about it. First of all, Hollister has a patent on this coating process, doesn't he? So how can McKee or anyone else use it even if they knew the formula? All Hollister would have to do is enforce his patent and he's protected. So what's the purpose?"

"Must be some benefit," Larry said. "Otherwise all this would be pointless, wouldn't it?"

"There's more," Cage said. "I don't believe McKee killed John Malone."

"What makes you say that?"

"McKee originally wanted me to bring Ben Hollister *and* Malone to wherever he plans on holding this meet."

"Maybe he was trying to fake you out."

"No, he really thought Malone was still alive. It caught him off guard, he had to hang up and think about it a couple minutes and call me back. He wasn't faking it, Larry. I could tell."

"Who else would have a motive?"

"Ben Hollister."

Larry gave him a questioning look.

"That's right," Cage said. "I'll bet he's been waiting for a chance to get rid of Malone for a long time. Then along comes Freeman McKee and, bingo, here's a golden opportunity to kill two birds with one stoneface. And he snookered me in for a stinking five hundred dollars."

"You don't know that for sure," Larry said. "I wouldn't expect the guy to come right out and admit he killed John Malone."

"Goddamn it Larry, I don't give a shit whether he would or not, all I want now is to get Caprita back. I've been driving around half the night thinking about this and the only hope I have of her coming out alive is by me doing everything this sonofabitch wants."

"I know how you feel, my friend. I can't help but think that could be Doris. But you can't believe Hollister is gonna go along with this. Which means you'd have to use force. Then you're no better than he is."

"Don't moralize with me, Larry, I'm not affected. I talked to the guy on the phone. McKee might be a killer, but I'm telling you he didn't do this one. My money's on Hollister. And if I'm right, as far as I'm concerned that makes him responsible."

"You're looking for a scapegoat," Larry said firmly. "You want him to be guilty so you can justify handing him over to McKee. You've tried and convicted him already. That's the last thing I would have expected from you."

"We're not talking courtroom etiquette here," Cage said, matching Larry's tone. "I'm not out to prepare an air tight case for a jury, I don't have the time. All I know is that every move Hollister made since I first showed up at that condo has been suspect, and right now that's good enough for me."

"I'm just saying you should back off and let the proper authorities handle it. That's the best chance Caprita has. You're too personally involved to rely totally on your own judgment. And don't forget the Bureau's now officially on the case. Take my word for it, if anybody can get Caprita back unharmed, it's them."

Cage gave him a straightforward look. "Would they die for her, Larry? Would they deliberately step in front of a bullet, or take the blade of a knife, or smother a bomb with their own body that was meant for her? Would they be that committed, Larry, willing to make that kind of sacrifice? I would."

Silence.

"Anyway, I can't take the chance of going to the police and have them get careless and tip off McKee. He'll kill her for sure."

Larry, resigned, finally spread his hands and said, "What do you want from me?"

"Information. Everything you can give me on Freeman McKee that might tell me something about what he is. His skills, his habits, his likes and dislikes ... anything that'll help me understand the bastard. You said the Bureau is building a file on him. I want to know what they know. Will you help me?"

"I'll talk to Jerry Culpepper and have it for you in the morning," he said without hesitation. "Or rather this morning. What else?"

"Back me up if I need it?"

"Of course."

"I appreciate it."

It was after 4:00 A.M. when he got back to the apartment. He stripped down to his shorts, cut off the lights and sat cross-legged on the living room floor in front of the lighted aquarium. He gazed absently at the fish, let his shoulders sag and took a dozen long deep breaths, letting them out slowly, trying to relieve the pressure cooker of tension and nerves. He was wired. He needed sleep, at least a few hours, to do what he had to do, so he followed a meandering angelfish, forced himself to visualize big fluffy clouds, gurgling streams, floating space debris. The light from the aquarium spilled around him like an aura as he gradually entered the level of consciousness taught to him years ago, when he'd owned the small carnival, back before the government made him a criminal. The man was a sideshow exhibit, called himself Wee Willie Wong, a short skinny Chinese who could turn his body into a human pretzel and claimed to be a direct descendent of Ming himself. Wee Willie kept a brilliantly colored Japanese betta fighting fish in a bowl and taught Cage how to, as he put it, "cleanse the soul and put it at peace." Willie said that to assume the relaxed position and focus on the "undulating fish" while conjuring up quiet scenes would "compel the raging spirit to acknowledge the movements of the peaceful fish and mimic its actions."

Cage had tried it before, when he was alone and didn't have to worry about looking like a fool, and he'd had some pleasant experiences that surprised him.

But not this time. No fish was about to calm this raging spirit. The visions of clouds, streams and space debris couldn't budge the image of Freeman McKee, couldn't erase the mental pictures he'd already formed about what might be happening to Caprita even while he was sitting here like a fucking Buddhist monk trying not to think about her.

He jumped up and went into the bathroom, ran the shower as hot as he could stand it, sat down in the tub with his back to the spray and let the water pound him, then showered and went to bed and buried his face in Caprita's pillow that smelled of Wind Song, her favorite scent and his, too. Grits leaped up beside him, sniffed at Caprita's empty spot, curled up and went to sleep.

But not Cage. Even attempting sleep in his present state was unthinkable, so he went back into the living room, turned the stereo on, lowered himself to the couch and listened to New Age in the dark. That was even worse, because they had listened to nearly every song together, and he cut it off after ten minutes, more wired than ever.

His private dinosaur reared up at him then. *You know what will do it, don't you? So what are you waiting for, go get it, you don't owe anybody any explanations. Without sleep you won't be worth a damn to yourself, much less Caprita.*

Cage went into the bedroom and took Caprita's old jewelry box down from the top shelf. Inside was a small sandwich bag with a quarter ounce of Humbolt County's best sessemilla that had remained untouched for nearly a year, ever since Cage just inexplicably lost his taste for it. Now it was a godsend.

He sat on the bed with the night lamp on and rolled a fat joint with fingers that trembled and spilled green pot leaves on the white sheets. He went to the kitchen for a book of matches and a mayonnaise cap for an ashtray, came back and lit up, sucking the smoke deep into his lungs. The smoke was so harsh he had to fight to keep it there. He took another hit and this one was easier, the third easier yet. His ears were ringing and his head grew heavy. Sometime later he became aware that he was sitting in bed staring at his bare feet, the half-smoked joint lying dead in the mayonnaise cap.

He fell back on her pillow, burrowed into it like before, surrounded himself with her scent, the marijuana helping him lull his senses into almost believing she was lying next to him . . .

Larry said, "Here it is, the whole nine yards," and dropped the manila envelope on the coffee table. It was 7:20 A.M., and Larry had wasted no time getting a copy of the case file the FBI was building on Freeman McKee.

Larry went to the kitchen for more coffee while Cage opened the envelope and removed a report bound in acetate that was thirty-one pages long, single-spaced, under the familiar letterhead of the FBI. Many of the pages had Magic Marker lines blacking out the identities of the agents conducting the interviews.

He raised his voice after Larry. "How did you get this so fast?"

"Know the right people," Larry called back. "It's a

personality profile put together by Research and Analysis. Includes a summary of his movements over the last ten years, or as close as they can put it together. The guy doesn't leave much of a trail. But people who meet him don't forget him."

"Any word on him yet?"

"They've checked the airlines, motels and rental car agencies, so far it's a blank. But that doesn't mean much. He'd know better than to use his own name."

Cage opened the file: Raised by a domineering mother with ambitions of being a rodeo performer. A brilliant CPA father whose journals and ledgers left him no time for fatherly functions. Interviews with friends and neighbors revealed a divided household where self-interest was the prevailing rule and social intimacy discouraged. As a family unit the McKees appeared to be totally dysfunctional.

Observations from teachers and other professional acquaintances painted Freeman as "emotionless and cruel, incapable of feeling empathy or love and with a total lack of regard for the welfare of others, often given to periodic episodes of aggressive or parasitic behavior." More like it. There were brief descriptions of the armadillo roasting and the kid with the broken wrist, a longer piece about the bathroom incident with Joe Odell that turned out not to have been exaggeration after all.

Cage skipped ahead until he came to a page with the heading SUMMARY OF MOVEMENTS.

Larry came out of the kitchen with a fresh cup and took a seat at the opposite end of the couch. He blew into the mug and sipped and let Cage read without interruption.

Using the FBI's sophisticated computer hookup and national crime reporting system, Research and Analysis had back-traced McKee to Miami, where he had his first run-in with the law. After a stint in jail he was suspected of joining a local rip-off gang called The Invaders but quickly dropped out of sight.

The next official entry had come from the Phoenix, Arizona, DA's Office seven months earlier, the one Larry had told him about. McKee had been charged with the kidnap/murder of a local jewelry store owner but had walked with the help of one of the city's top criminal defense lawyers. The M.O. used to restrain the jewelry store owner, the use of baling twine intricately secured with "double slipknots," triggered a computer response that had recognized this same M.O. from the Bronx homicide that took place ten years earlier. The computers said the probability that the same man had restrained both victims was an eighty-six percent certainty—which was nowhere near good enough to justify a warrant, especially since McKee had been acquitted of the Phoenix murder.

At the time of his arrest, McKee had a carbon copy of a Mexicali Air Lines plane ticket from Guaymas, Mexico, to Phoenix, Arizona dated three days before the jeweler's murder. Subsequent investigations conducted through Mexican authorities revealed that McKee had arrived in Guaymas by train from Mexico City in July of 1981 (six days after the Bronx killing). He had a lot of money and claimed that he had won a lottery in the United States. He placed a little of it in the right local hands and gained permanent residency status by simply buying a fishing boat and a business license. He also bought a modest hacienda on Ave. Aquiles Serdan, just north of the city on the road to Hermosillo. He hired a part-time maid to care for the hacienda and a two-man crew to operate the forty-two-foot Grand Banks he'd paid eighty thousand for but never once turned a profit with, and there went another six or eight grand a year.

But it was cheap to live in Guaymas, where the average annual income was equivalent to nine hundred Yankee dollars, and McKee was apparently flush, so he continued to operate in the red, chipping away at the small fortune he brought with him by indulging in such luxuries as maintaining a steady supply of young Guaymas girls. An FBI agent from the Santa Fe field office had actually flown to Guaymas and interviewed two of the girls known to have been regular guests of McKee and who claimed he'd once shown them a video of him committing a murder.

The victim had been a local fisherman named José De Balistros, who had allegedly set fire to McKee's boat, causing it to be put in dry dock for two weeks of repairs. The girls said that the video showed the man lying bound on the foredeck of McKee's boat, which he'd named *Destiny*, being slowly garroted to death by McKee, who had looped a hundred-pound test-line around the Mexican's neck and was twisting it tight with a marlinspike. The girls said they could hear the man's death gurgles while he thrashed about, then became still. They said that McKee then tied a boat anchor to the man and rolled him off into a thousand feet of open water. They said the man had been bound with brown twine that bent him backward like a bow.

Eventually McKee made the acquaintance of a Honduran national named Chee Chee Sandoval who ran a mid-sized coke-smuggling operation out of Cuidad Obregon, fifty miles southeast of Guaymas. Sandoval took a liking to Freeman McKee, calling him "the quiet American with the frozen face," and would occasionally give him consignments of packaged cocaine to ferry five hundred miles up the Gulf to Puerto Peñazco. According to informants, McKee would turn the product over to others, who would then truck the shipment forty miles to Sonoíta, where it would eventually be smuggled into Arizona via a secret tunnel that was supposed to exist somewhere along the three-hundred-mile border between Nogales and San Luis.

According to the report, McKee proved to be diligent and loyal, and it was said that he had returned from one such trip with an arrogant fifteen-year-old bandit who had been caught taping explosives to the hull of the *Destiny* shortly after it entered Puerto Peñazco. Some credit the story to Sandoval himself, how he was suitably impressed with McKee's powers of persuasion in convincing the reluctant kid to name his employer by tying him to a workbench and forcing his head into a vice. It was claimed that McKee had continued tightening the vice even after the kid had screamed out the entire contents of his memory banks ...and then had taken the body out to the middle of the Gulf, secured it with an anchor and hundred-pound test-line and dropped it overboard. McKee allegedly endeared himself further to Sandoval by personally eliminating the employer, a rival named García-Luis Rodriguez, by inverting a galvanized bucket filled with wet cement over his head and letting it dry before taking the body out to join the kid.

McKee moved up fast after that, becoming Sandoval's most trusted and reliable *sicario*—hired assassin. He came and went with the wind, dropping from sight for days at a time, reportedly tracking down and systematically dispatching the enemies of Chee Chee Sandoval.

And then, eight months ago, it had all caught up with him. For reasons still unknown, Sandoval fell out of favor with the Colombian cartels, who promptly sent more than a hundred of their own *sicarios* into Cuidad Obregon in the dead of night to conduct simultaneous raids against his ranch and two warehouses. A half-dozen other assassins were directed to take care of McKee; three to his hacienda outside Guaymas, three to the *Destiny* riding anchor in the harbor. When the shooting had stopped, there were nine dead at the ranch, including Chee Chee Sandoval, and five more at the warehouses. They gutted McKee's hacienda with grenades and automatic weapons fire, but McKee hadn't been there. They did the same with the *Destiny*, but McKee hadn't been there either. Later it was discovered that while his boat was being destroyed, McKee had been four blocks away in the Hotel Impala, spending the night with his favorite call girl. He reportedly slipped away before dawn, barely escaping with his life and leaving behind all his worldly possessions.

Three days later he turned up again, this time in Phoenix, Arizona.

Cage finished reading the report, looked up at Larry. "I'm impressed, I guess."

"I wanted you to be," Larry said. "I still wish you'd let the Bureau handle this. Give the girl her best shot—"

"No. I can't take that chance. I'm taking a big enough one having you come by."

"What about Hollister?"

"I'm seeing him today. I haven't worked it all out yet, but I'm laying everything face up on the table for him. I figure he's guilty but I'll know more when we're eyeball to eyeball. After that I'm a little murky on details."

"You know I can't just stand by and let you commit a felony."

"What felony?"

"Cut the shit. Listen, that girl means almost as

much to me as she does to you. But I won't let you swap Ben Hollister for her. And contrary to your suspicions—and that's all they are—*I'm* still operating on the premise that McKee took out John Malone and now wants you to deliver Hollister like some . . . some sacrificial lamb. I want you to know it can't happen that way. Hey, what the hell do you expect to do, anyway, lead a charge against the castle and rescue her all by yourself? You're not the damn cavalry, you know."

"I don't plan on acting like the cavalry," Cage said. "More like the Trojan Horse."

CHAPTER THIRTEEN

The voice that came out of the call box sounded close to hysteria.

"Who's there?"

"It's me, Ben, Allen Cage. Like to talk to you a minute, if it's alright."

After a moment Ben said, "At eight-thirty in the morning?"

"If you don't mind."

Another short wait, then the door buzzed and Cage went in, took the elevator to the eighteenth floor and was met outside PH–2 by a black uniformed guard who kept his eyes on Cage and his hand on the butt of his holstered revolver while he tapped on the door. The decal on the sleeve of his starched khaki shirt said BenJohn Electronics, Inc—Security.

The door opened and Ben Hollister was standing there in blue walking shorts and a blue and gold UCLA football jersey. He said, "Good job, Douglas, thanks. Come on in, Allen."

He took Cage into the kitchen, saying to excuse the mess and asking if he wanted a cup of coffee. Cage said yes, black would be fine, and pulled up a chair. He watched Ben carefully as he poured coffee into a delicate teacup and brought it to him, keeping up the conversation as he went.

"I haven't been out of this place going on two days now," Ben said, "and I'm not budging till I hear Freeman McKee's ass is buried in a cell. Christ, I can still see that fucking monkey grinning at me, John with his head back and his eyes bugging out. You can see I pulled one of my security people ... two of 'em, actually, one stationed outside that door twenty-four hours a day for the duration. Tell you the truth, I was all set to get out of here period, but I figured that might be going a little overboard."

Ben sat down and stirred his coffee. He lifted the cup and sipped, placed it back on the saucer, sighed and looked at Cage. "Now then," he said pleasantly, "what can I do for you?"

Cage said, "Ben, is there any reason why you'd want to kill John Malone?"

For maybe three seconds, Ben Hollister looked at him without speaking, forehead knitted into a frown, then said, "What the hell is that supposed to mean?"

He sounded sincere, but Cage had caught the momentary tightening of the lips, and even now the man's face was two shades lighter than before he'd asked the question. He hadn't been able to control that. But was it brought on by a guilty conscience, or by the revelation that he was suddenly a suspect? Cage couldn't be sure.

"It means just what it sounds like, Ben. Now give me a yes or no answer."

"Are you thinking I killed my own partner?"

"Yes or no."

149

"*No*, goddamn it! Now answer me."

Cage still wasn't sure. Ben was indignant, trying to stare him down, giving an award-winning performance if it was an act.

"That idea has been mentioned," Cage said. "Because if you did, then having Freeman McKee force his way in here the other night was perfect timing. And if that were the case, then hiring me was a genius stroke. For one, it let you document the fact through an outside party that McKee actually did break in here. For another, it gave you the opportunity to paint the guy as a psycho and show how terrified you guys were of him. It would also explain why you didn't call the police. You didn't want him picked up. Not then."

"How come you're talking like this is all fact?" Ben demanded.

"Just being hypothetical. Playing devil's advocate."

"Well, it doesn't play here, my friend. I don't find a fucking thing about it that's either informative or amusing. John Malone and I grew up together, went through high school and college together, went into business together. He was my fucking best friend. And on top of that, this Detective Evers calls me last night to warn me that Freeman's suspected of other killings and advises me to be extremely careful. Like who don't know that. I suppose it was a stroke of luck the bastard turned out to be a homicidal maniac too, huh? Try getting somebody to buy that shit for one minute, Cage."

"Somebody already has bought it."

"Sure—*you*. If it was anybody with the police, *they'd* be here. And what brought on this change of attitude anyway?"

"Freeman McKee kidnapped my fiancée yesterday," Cage said quietly. "He felt like I was challenging him the other night and now he's using her to get to me."

Ben ran a hand across his face and looked away. "Oh, Jesus Christ...man, I'm sorry. I never should have got you into this. I just didn't know..."

His voice trailed off and he sat there shaking his head.

"He called me last night," Cage said. "He wants me to do something before he'll let Caprita go. If he plans on letting her go at all."

"What's that?"

"Something personal. Your friend's very imaginative. I told him about John Malone."

Ben's worry lines came back. "I bet the crazy fucker crowed about it, didn't he?"

"No. He said he didn't do it."

"You were maybe expecting him to confess?"

Ben sighed and leaned forward. "Look, Allen, I can't begin to tell you how bad I feel about your fiancée. If there's anything I can do—I mean *any*thing—just say the word. But the only thing I'm responsible for is hiring you, and if you want to count that, then I got no defense. But that's all I'm guilty of, man. I swear it."

Larry had been right. He was too personally involved to be making judgment calls, having a hard time being objective. He'd come here filled with conviction, having thought it all out the night before from behind the wheel of his Cougar. But now he didn't know. Maybe Larry was right about the rest of it, too. Maybe he *did* want the guy to be guilty and was reading the signs to support that opinion. Cage decided to feed him a little more and see what happened.

"I was telling you McKee wanted me to do something before he'd let Caprita go?"

"Yeah?"

"What he wanted me to do was force you to give up the chemical composition of that computer chip coating you discovered."

Ben's mouth fell open and an expression of pure relief sent the worry lines fading.

"Shit, is that all? He wants the chemical composition for Duracon-L? Wait right here."

Ben got up and left, came back a couple minutes later with a four-month-old edition of Business Week. He dropped it in front of Cage and sat.

"Page sixteen," he said. "It's a four-column piece called 'BenJohn Claims Patent Infringement On New Coating Compound'. That's it, right there. In a nutshell, what it's about is my old employer TRW developing a generic coating that duplicates my Duracon-L process step for step. The bastards still think it's theirs regardless of what the court said."

"What's this have to do with what we're talking about?" Cage asked.

"Turn the page."

Cage turned the page and picked up the story again.

"Take a look at that sidebar," Ben said, and pointed to a shaded box in the middle of the page that was divided into two columns. The first column was headed TRW'S "R–54." The second was headed BENJOHN'S "DURACON-L."

"Those are comparisons between my product and the process used by TRW to make the one they developed. I slapped a lawsuit on their asses and they settled out of court, agreed to stop making it. Shit, it's never been a big secret, both formulas are spelled out right there. All he had to do was buy a magazine."

Cage scanned the lists of unpronouncable names and strange symbols. Why in hell did McKee go through all this trouble to learn something that was obviously public knowledge? Maybe he only wanted Ben Hollister after all and was just trying to throw him off.

Forget motives for now. First he had to find Caprita. And that meant he would have to deliver Ben Hollister.

The man was practically beaming at him now, saying, "There you are, case closed. Copy it on a piece of paper and give it to the crazy sonofabitch. I suggest you have a squad of cops behind you when you do."

Ben pushed back his chair and stood. "Now if you'll excuse me," he said, "I've got a lot of phone calls to make. A couple of 'em concern John. His folks asked me to make arrangements to ship his body back to Houston. Not very pleasant, but like they say, somebody's got to do it. I wish you luck, Allen, I really do. If you need anything else from me, give me a call."

Cage took the elevator back to the lobby, the magazine sticking out of his back pocket, went out through the double doors to the guest parking area and got in the Cougar. He waited a while before leaving, face tilted up at the eighteenth floor, wishing again he could be certain about Ben Hollister. It wasn't yet beyond a reasonable doubt, but most of the evidence was against him, and Cage held on to that thought like a drowning victim would hold on to a raft, using it to justify his decision. He told himself there was no way he'd jeopardize Ben Hollister's safety and lead him into the lion's den if it wasn't a pretty good bet that he'd killed John Malone.

His private dinosaur reared up and said, *Who are you kidding?*

*   *   *

153

Brenda Alworth shoved the file drawer closed and walked back to her desk as Cage came in the front door.

"Larry said to tell you he's in back," she said. "You two are starting to spend an awful lot of time back there lately. What's the big mystery?"

"Did I get any calls this morning?"

"Not yet. Expecting any?"

"Just asking."

"Seriously, Allen, is something wrong? You both look as though you were ready to kill, and Larry hasn't said two sentences since he came in. Are you two fighting or something?"

"Not now, Olive Oil, okay? Do me that one favor and don't ask any questions."

She shrugged and turned to her computer. "Well, excuse me. Are you taking any calls?"

"Only if his name is Freeman McKee."

Cage stuck the copy of Business Week in the bottom drawer of his desk and stopped off at the Silex for a cup of coffee, then went through the curtain and found Larry with the stool pulled close to the workbench, calibrating the frequency on the receiving unit of a wireless transponder.

Larry looked at him. "Well? You see him?"

"I saw him."

"And?"

"I think he did it."

"But you're not positive."

"No. How can I be without the guy copping out? But it's the only thing that works."

"Yeah, right. So how'd you approach him?"

"Asked him straight out if he had any reason to kill John Malone. He got real outraged at that and went on the offensive. But I'll tell you, Larry, the guy's face drained when I sprung it on him."

"That's not too surprising, mine would drain too. I still think you're off base."

Cage was glad he'd decided not to show Larry the Business Week piece. He would jump all over it to support his argument, saying it was proof that McKee really wanted Ben Hollister and was using this nonsense about Duracon-L as a cover.

Goddamn, he could even be right about that too.

Larry said, "You're gonna give him Hollister, aren't you? All this talk about guilt or innocence doesn't even get taken into consideration."

"Sure it does. It'll decide how aggressive I'll be if he balks at my idea. Goddamn it, Larry, what do you want me to do? I might not be a hundred percent sure Hollister's guilty, but I'm a thousand percent sure that Caprita is in major trouble. Now what side do you think I'm gonna come down on? If it's any consolation, I'll be right with him."

Larry wiped his hands on a paper towel, swung around on the stool and faced Cage. "I'll tell you what kind of consolation that is," he said, "It's *bull*shit. Unless Hollister takes some perverse pleasure in having you die with him."

"I think we'd have a better than even chance," Cage said. "I've got this guy pegged now, Larry. I know what he'll do and I know how to prepare for him—"

"So do I."

Cage had been afraid of that.

Larry turned back to the transponder. "By hooking you up to this."

Cage was caught off-balance. "I thought you were all set to put your foot down. What changed your mind?"

"Because the only way I'll be able to keep you from going through with this is by putting you in jail, and considering your track record I wouldn't feel too confident even then. So I'm doing what I hope is the next best thing and try to establish some measure of control. With luck maybe we can get out of this without anyone getting killed. Maybe. But you have to let me call the shots. I like to think I'm a little more rational than you are right now, even if it isn't by much. Now that's the best deal you're gonna get, so take it or leave it."

"Larry, you're forgetting how I told you the guy acted on the phone. He's confident enough not to even worry about a trace, and I believe he was checking the power load. If he takes those kind of precautions to check for phone taps, doesn't it figure he'd do the same for a body wire?"

"He won't find this one," Larry said. "Paul designed it. The transmitter is fitted into the shell of a Timex wristwatch with a signal booster that gives it an effective range of two miles, depending on the terrain. I should be able to keep within that distance, if he doesn't pick you up in a helicopter."

Larry opened a small leather case and removed an innocent-looking Timex Ironman wristwatch with a Velcro band. He handed it to Cage.

"I don't think he'd suspect this, do you? The antenna wire runs through the band."

Cage was already shaking his head no. "No way. He could pick up the signal with a hand-held detector."

"Not with this one, he won't. You activate the signal by pushing the lap and stopwatch buttons simultaneously. You can do that even if he uses restraints—they're very sensitive. But you don't do it till he's checked for a wire or you're sure he's not going to. He's calling you again tonight with instructions where to bring Hollister, right?"

Cage put the Timex in his pocket. "That's what he said."

"Then when he does, you call me here and tell me when and where the meet's taking place. I'll get there early and check it out for the best spot to receive. And don't worry, he won't spot me. Neither will you."

Cage still wasn't sold, but it didn't look like Larry was going to give him any alternatives. Hell, it just might work at that. Unless for some reason he couldn't activate the signal.

Which wouldn't make him any worse off than he already was.

"One condition," Cage said. "No one else gets involved. I want your word on that."

"You've got it. If we're gonna make it happen, we have to work together."

"Then let's do it," Cage said.

Larry looked at him again. "I'm not asking how you plan on getting Hollister to do this, and I'm sure I don't want to know. But I'm going to assume it's voluntary."

Sure he was. "It would be kind of hard getting him out of that penthouse with an armed guard outside the door any other way," Cage said.

Larry raised his eyebrows. "Armed guard, huh?"

"Don't say it, Larry, he could have just as easy done it for show. Doesn't prove a thing."

"Uh huh."

Cage wanted to get back to his apartment. He wanted to sit and think and watch the telephone, his umbilical cord to Caprita. He wanted to prepare for Freeman McKee.

He said, "Well, I better get back. There's always the chance he could call early."

"I'll be right here," Larry reminded him.

Cage stuffed his hands in his pockets and looked off. "Larry, I know how much this goes against your grain and what kind of risk you're taking if it blows up in our laps. Regardless of the outcome, I want you to know you're a damn good friend."

"Yes, I am," Larry said. "And as a damn good friend I want to leave you with something else to think about"

Cage waited.

"You'd better be damn sure that McKee does want to hang on to you for a little while. Because if he doesn't and decides you've fulfilled your purpose in life, he's gonna leave you right there. And if he does, we can kiss goodbye all hope of ever seeing Caprita alive again. At least I can kiss it goodbye. It won't matter to you."

CHAPTER FOURTEEN

Alone again, bound and gagged as before. Cassette recorder on the nightstand turning silently, memorizing every sound. At least the TV was on a normal channel now, she thought it was ESPN, but the volume was off. Sleek race cars hurtling down empty city streets lined with waving spectators, the effect diminished by the absence of cheers and roaring engines. Occasionally she would focus her attention on the screen and pick a favorite, temporarily taking her mind off the ache in her right cheek bone and the maddening itch beneath the tape covering her mouth.

How long had he been gone this time? He'd been in and out often during the day, but usually for no more than twenty or thirty minutes at a time. Twice he'd returned with food, but only once did he offer her any—a greasy hamburger and wilted dill pickle, which she managed to choke down with a Mountain Dew solely because it allowed her restraints to be removed. He had allowed her two additional trips to the bathroom, probably because he didn't want her wetting the bed, making her leave the door ajar so he could see her reflection in the mirror. Knowing his eyes were on her had caused her skin to prickle and made her feel like taking a bath, which was obviously out of the question.

He seemed to enjoy listening to her talk, so he left the tape off her mouth whenever he was in the room. He would sit sideways at the table with his arms and legs crossed, partially shadowed by the changing light from the TV, and ask her to tell him a little about herself. She'd read somewhere that the more a hostage could personalize herself with her abductor the more likely she was to survive, the theory being that you had to make the kidnapper see you as a person instead of an object.

So she'd talked his ear off, stretching it a bit by stating that she'd always wanted to be a nurse and relieve pain and suffering. If she wanted to make him see her as a person, she might as well as try for Mother Teresa. The man had listened quietly, never interrupting, leading her deeper into herself with patient encouragement whenever she faltered or tried to evade a subject. He was like a goddamn psychiatrist conducting a therapy session, gently probing and prodding in a neutral voice, steering the conversation in directions of interest to *him.*

Like sex. He'd wanted to know her first experience. How old was she, where did it take place, did she enjoy it. She had answered without wavering, making it sound trivial: she was seventeen, it was three days after her senior prom with a boy she thought she loved but never thought she'd see again because she was going away to Allegheny College in Pennsylvania in the fall. As for did she enjoy it, she told him it was pleasant enough, but nothing like you read in the romance novels.

He wanted to know about Allen. What kind of work did he do, what special training had he received, what were his hobbies. She said that he sold electrical equipment and let it go at that, hoping he wouldn't press the issue. He was just a normal guy, she said, a weekend sports junkie who liked to munch in front of the TV, spend a day at the beach, go to an occasional movie if it wasn't too long. No special training, unless you counted his boast to be the best barbecue chef west of Illinois. But she missed him, she said, and she certainly hoped they could get this ironed out soon so she could get back home to him.

No comment.

Caprita came alert at the sound of voices outside the door. A man and woman, she believed, arguing as they came nearer, feet crunching on what she already knew was a gravel driveway. She could hear what they were saying now, the man complaining about the amount of money he was laying out for what would be maybe ten minutes of pleasure. The woman was telling him he wasn't committed yet, he could turn right around and take her back to the China Club if he was having second thoughts...

Now they were on the concrete walkway, the woman's high heels tapping along at a rapid pace.

Caprita glanced at the recorder sitting ominously on the nightstand. Could she risk trying to attract the couple's attention as they passed right by the door? All she could do was moan loudly through her nose, which had only a minor chance of success and would most certainly be picked up on the tape. Even if they did hear her, chances were they would mistake the sound for passion.

The voices and high heels grew louder as they drew abreast of the door...then receded as they moved away while Caprita listened in frustration, remembering the man's warning to drown her in the toilet if she tried signaling for help.

She turned her face away and into the pillow. *Allen ...God, where are you?*

It was 7:05 when he got the call. Cage snatched up the receiver on the first ring.

"Hello?"

"Hi, clown," Freeman said. "Just a sec."

A brief silence, Cage picturing McKee sticking a needlelike probe into the phone cord, letting the digital display tell him how much power was coming through the line.

Freeman came back on. "Okay, you all set to take care of business?"

"Yes."

"No tricks? Not that I think you'd tell me if you had any, I'm just reminding you about the nurse. Now when I come to meet you and Hollister, if I don't get back to her inside a couple hours, she's gonna die a very horrible death. I mean what I say."

"I want you to bring her with you," Cage said. "I want to be able to see she's all right."

"You'll have to take my word for that, I'm not bringing her anywhere. I told you the plan and that's the way we'll do it, no negotiations."

Cage's jaw tightened and he counted to three. "Then tell me what you want me to do. But keep in mind that Hollister has an armed guard outside his door twenty-four hours a day now, scared to death you're gonna show up and do to him what you did to John

Malone. He says he's not budging until they pick you up."

"Looks like you got your work cut out for you, then. But you'll find a way. I could."

"Sure, you're an expert." It wouldn't hurt to stroke him.

"I got a feeling you've been around the block a few times yourself," Freeman said.

Cage couldn't help it, he had to ask. His private dinosaur was demanding more information, acknowledging for the first time the possibility that when push came to shove, he might have a problem delivering a potentially innocent man for almost certain execution.

Cage said, "Hey, McKee? Help me out here, will you? I'm not feeling very good with myself right now."

"Conscience bothering you, huh? I figured a tough guy like you would be above that. But I want you to be dedicated and believe in what you're doing, so I'm gonna prove to your satisfaction that I wasn't anywhere near that condo when John Malone went down. Would that give you a higher opinion of yourself and inspire you not to blow it?"

Cage said, "It would."

"Then listen to this, clown. According to the papers, Malone died sometime between seven and seven-thirty in the morning, am I right?"

"Right."

"Couldn't have been me, then. I was following your girlfriend, and I can prove it. She left the apartment at seven-o-five. She's halfway to the carport when you come bopping out in a gray sweatshirt waving a pair of sunglasses at her. She turns back to meet you, laughing and shaking her head and shit, takes the glasses and gives you a sweet peck on the cheek. Sound familiar? Otherwise, I would've snatched her on the spot."

It sure did sound familiar. It also gave new life to the quiet rage he'd had to suppress with McKee, and for the moment he couldn't trust himself to speak.

"I'll take that as a yes," Freeman said. "She made a stop for gas at an ARCO station on National Boulevard, then another stop at Winchell's Donuts on Wilshire before getting to the hospital at seven-fifty. Wilshire Memorial. You're just gonna have to take my word again on this last part, but I promise you that was her route."

He believed that too. Caprita took turns with several other nurses stopping by Winchell's every day, and the ARCO station on National was their usual place for gas. McKee had been there, all right, and he'd followed her all the way to Wilshire Memorial. There was no possible way he could have killed John Malone.

Cage said, "Tell me when and where you want him."

"Feel a lot better now, do you?"

Silence.

"Good. Then listen up. I want you to bring that little lizard to the rest station at Zuma Beach, have him there at four o'clock tomorrow morning."

"Four A.M.? Look, McKee, I don't think you understand. I have to trick him out of that condo to get to him, unless you want me to shoot it out with his bodyguard, and I'm no Wyatt Earp. Why can't you pick a normal hour?"

"Traffic. I hate this L.A. traffic. Four o'clock. Park right next to the men's room, cut the engine and wait. You know where it is? About a quarter mile past the Zuma Beach sign, off Pacific Coast Highway."

"I know it," Cage said. Last year he and Caprita

had gone scuba diving offshore at just about that same location. "When do I get her?"

"Soon as I verify the information. I'd say an hour or two."

"What happens after I hand over Hollister?"

"You go back home and wait for the nurse to call you, if everything's on the up and up. You hold a memorial service for her if I even suspect it isn't."

"I told you I'd keep my end and I will," Cage said. "I'll have Ben Hollister in Zuma Beach at four o'clock tomorrow morning."

"What about the bodyguard?"

"I can work around him. But remember, you need me to dig Hollister out of his hole, and I will. Just don't bother the woman, okay?"

"Four o'clock, clown. Don't keep me waiting. Use your car so I'll recognize you."

Click.

Cage hung up slowly, his mind off on a tangent, and almost set the phone on the nonexistent coffee table, some of the more stubborn fragments still ground into the carpet. Caprita would raise hell with him for that. Maybe he ought to get the Dust Buster and get down on his hands and knees and give it a good going over before she got home and cut her foot or something, the way she always liked to slide down on the sofa and run her toes through the soft pile.

He slammed the phone on the end table hard enough to send Grits dashing into the kitchen. He stood and began circling the room, cracking his knuckles and thinking how he'd been right all along, fighting a running battle with his private dinosaur to keep from rushing over to the Marina that minute and . . .

He had to sit down again. He leaned his head

against the sofa back and called up the file he'd read on Freeman McKee. Everyone who had gotten on the man's wrong side had turned up dead, most often leaving behind the killer's distinctive "signature" of expertly knotted baling twine and broken necks. Freeman liked to drag it out, give his victims time to appreciate their predicament, because all you had to do was look at the guy for five seconds, then listen to him for another five, and you'd realize that this one would bear watching even among friends, if he had any. He had an ego as big as a battle tank and almost as destructive, and he wouldn't tolerate any assault against it.

Freeman McKee. Cage recognized him now, though the memory had been dimmed by culture change. You could find him in every penitentiary in the country, and they all had one thing in common. Killing was their first option, not their last.

McKee would never allow him to live. But first he would want to mollify his bruised ego by showing Cage how tough he was.

Cage waited ten minutes before calling Banes and Twiford. He wasn't concerned about McKee tapping his phone. It was too dangerous. But he didn't put it past the devious bastard to call back a minute or so later to see if the line was busy.

When Larry answered, he said, "Zuma Beach, four o'clock tomorrow morning, are you ready for that?"

"He didn't do us any favors, did he?" Larry said. "It's wide open out there, especially that time of morning with hardly nothing moving. Gives him a good view, if he also happens to have night goggles."

"I don't like it, Larry, the guy's too wily."

" 'Wily'? Don't choke on me now, buddy, we're getting close. The good thing is we won't have to worry about signal diversions. I'll check it out. Unless I call you back, assume I'm in place."

"Larry?"

"Yeah?"

"If this works out the way it's supposed to, I'm trusting you to do the right thing."

"And what would that be?"

"Short of risking you or Caprita, I want you to do everything in your power, call on every piece of Academy training you ever learned, and keep Freeman McKee alive. Will you do that for me, Larry?"

After a pause, Larry said, "Let's concentrate on Caprita right now, okay?"

"I need it, Larry. I really do need it like you wouldn't believe."

"Yes, I would," he said.

Freeman held his finger on the hook and surveyed Hollywood Boulevard from the phone kiosk at Hollywood and Wilcox and thought, So much for the clown. Now for the ringmaster.

He dialed a Phoenix exchange, waited for the operator to tell him how much to deposit, then waited again while the call went through and a professional female voice answered.

"Nine-one-four-one."

Freeman said, "Mr. Singer, please."

"I'll have to page him. Name, please."

Freeman told her.

"Number?"

Freeman gave it to her.

"Thank you," she said, and broke the connection.

Freeman hung up and gave Hollyweird Boulevard another cursory inspection while he waited. He could entertain himself a great deal just by watching the foot traffic that passed, the homos, lesbos, creepos and just plain assholes in every kind of perverted getup you could imagine. What a place. They should go ahead and drop one of those neutron bombs that killed people but left buildings standing and start all over again. Give him Texas anytime, where you could finger-walk your way up a silky thigh in a dark bar without worrying about grabbing a pecker bigger than yours.

He didn't like this mystery man shit one bit, and if Freeman hadn't known instantly that this was it, the ultimate destiny he'd always searched for and knew was waiting for him somewhere, he would have told the guy to take a flying leap. Well, they said fate was fickle.

There he'd been, about to go on trial for his life after screwing up royally on the jeweler job, two stinking transients ready to testify they'd seen him come out of the store. The biggest jackpot he'd ever been in, even bigger than losing damn near two million dollars when everything blew up around him in Mexico and made him an instant pauper. Then, here comes lawyer Daniel Johnstone-Kelly, a short Irishman in a shiny black suit who showed up to visit him one day. Freeman at first thought he was an undertaker sent by the state to take his measurements, that's how sure they were of their case, so he was twice relieved when the man identified himself and said he'd been hired to represent him by a client who wished to remain anonymous.

"Why would somebody do that for me?" Freeman wanted to know, and the man had said, "Because my client is going to ask you to do him a favor in return. It will be a mutual accommodation."

The lawyer explained that his nameless client had been following his case in the media and became impressed with the way he'd maintained his composure and kept his mouth shut. His client could use such a man to negotiate some "rather delicate" business on his behalf, business that would best be conducted without his client being identified. Freeman asked what kind of business, and the lawyer had said he didn't know and didn't want to know, his job was to use all of his considerable ability to show a jury reasonable doubt so the state wouldn't unjustly execute him. Now did Freeman want him to do that or didn't he?

The trial lasted four days, and when it was over it took the jury exactly two hours and fifty-seven minutes to reach a not-guilty verdict and send Freeman back into society. Daniel Johnstone-Kelly put him up at the Ramada Inn, paid a month in advance and gave him fifteen hundred dollars cash for what he called "walking-around money" while he got used to the outside again. He said his client would contact him in a day or so and would introduce himself as Mr. Singer. In the meantime he should relax, get laid, do whatever made him happy and wait for his client to call. Consider it a paid vacation, he'd said.

That night Freeman went out and bludgeoned a transient to death with a three-foot section of plumbing pipe behind the Oakwood Gardens Apartments on East Twenty-Sixth Street. He hit him a hundred and twenty-six times, one for each day he'd spent in jail, and when he returned to his room at the Ramada Inn after two in the morning, he put out the "Do Not Disturb" sign and slept eleven hours straight. He was finally awakened by the ringing telephone, and it had been the man—

The pay phone was ringing now, snapping Freeman out of his space walk. He picked it up. "Yeah?"

"This is Mr. Singer," the voice said. "Who am I speaking with, please?"

The guy always did that, putting a lot of bass in his voice so he could sound sinister. You'd think he was in a fucking John Le Carré novel or something. Who'd he expect to answer after getting his message?

"Freeman."

"Hello, Freeman. And how are you this evening? I hope you have some welcome news for me."

"I've got what they call good news and bad news," Freeman said. "Which one do you want first?"

"I'm not paying you fifty thousand dollars to give me bad news. I'm paying you to follow my instructions to the letter and get results. Now what's going on?"

Oh, man, did this motherfucker ever have a mouth on him, or what. Before this was all over . . .

Freeman said, "The bad news is John Malone went and got himself killed, and I didn't have anything to do with it."

"How?"

Freeman gave him a brief account, leaving out that he was the primary suspect.

"Now, isn't that a coincidence." Mr. Singer said, not sounding happy at all. "You may have endangered this entire project."

"I told you I didn't do it, and that's all I have to say on the subject. We still got Hollister, and he's the main one."

"You have him now?"

"No. But I will by the time you wake up in the morning."

"Is that definite?"

"As definite as I can be."

The man seemed to think about that for a while, then said, "In that case, we're still on course, just minus one. You're right, Malone isn't important. He would have had to go anyway."

Freeman said, "You're still gonna let me coax the information out of him, right?"

"Didn't I say I would, Freeman? I keep my promises."

"Then how about bringing my money when you come."

"I'll bring you half, like we agreed. The other half will be sent to your P.O. box in Phoenix as soon as I get back. Now where are you?"

The man just wouldn't stop using that demanding tone, would he? Feeling he could get away with it because he would still have twenty-five thousand dollars of Freeman's money. Only Freeman was coming dangerously close to writing off the second twenty-five grand and exercising his fantasies with Mr. Singer. Hell, it would almost be worth it. But now he had to keep him happy ... *Yazsuh, boss, anything you say, boss, don't press your luck, boss ...*

"Out on North La Cienega," Freeman said, "Adult motel called Eros, except it's got make-believe log cabins instead of rooms. You go past the office and follow the driveway, it kind of winds off to the left through a small stand of baby pines. Go all the way to the end and it's the last cabin on the right, number twenty-one. Nice and private. Finally gonna get to meet you, huh?"

"Don't sound so pleased, I'll be wearing a disguise. And I'm not staying a minute longer than it takes to get what I want from Ben Hollister and let him know who's persecuting him. You can take it from there."

So it wasn't all just business, then. The man had a personal score to settle as well. Freeman could understand vengeance, knew it as a great motivator, and he was curious to find out what his old buddy Ben Hollister had done to warrant the supreme penalty. He'd soon find out.

171

Mr. Singer said, "I want to know exactly when you're going to have Hollister there. Must be pretty early if it's before I get up in the morning. I'm on my second cup of coffee by six."

"I'll have him before it perks."

"Very good, Freeman," the man said. Like he was praising a two-year-old after taking his first potty shit. "That's the kind of news I like to hear. Why don't I just plan on having that second cup of coffee with you in the morning instead of by myself. Such a peaceful time of day, isn't it? I'll make myself at home while you talk to your friend."

Man, this guy belonged on a stage.

"Use a key and tap on the knob instead of the door so I'll know it's you," Freeman said, realizing he didn't have a clue what Mr. Singer looked like even without a disguise.

"Good thinking, Freeman. I like that."

"I thought it would appeal to you."

Mr. Singer said, "See you at six, then. And Freeman. When I get there, I don't want to find out that Ben Hollister also had a mysterious bout with death. I want him alive and conscious, Freeman. Or I am going to be very upset."

The man hung up.

Freeman placed the receiver gently on the hook and listened to his change drop into the coin box . . . and thought, *That did it*. Fuck the other twenty-five thousand, he was going to get off on Mr. Super-Mouth Singer. The guy probably had plans to shaft him anyway, go back to Phoenix and never let Freeman hear from him again. What could he do about it?

He left the phone kiosk and walked to his car that was parked in a red zone at the curb. He got in and thumbed two Rolaids from the roll lying on the console, popped them one at a time into his mouth and chewed while he meditated.

Freeman swore he'd almost had an out-of-body experience when Mr. Singer first told him who the subjects were. He'd undergone *some* sort of metaphysical change, that was for sure. The man said he'd done some deep background checking and discovered that Freeman went to the same high school as the two guys he was interested in. Ben Hollister and John Malone. Did he know them?

That's when the change came over him and it seemed as if he were floating upward in the midst of a gray cloud surrounded by a thousand winking fireflies, and for a few seconds he'd had difficulty breathing. Then everything gradually faded and he was returned to the present by Mr. Singer's voice saying softly, "Freeman? You still there, Freeman? I hope they weren't friends of yours. Because I'm going to ask you to do something really mean to them."

Friends? Not even close. Acquaintances, that was all. Friends didn't try to shy away from you, didn't lie to you, didn't call you names behind your back. Oh, he knew about the Stoneface jokes. Couldn't help but know, what with all the little suckasses that wanted to make Brownie points by being the first to tell him. But he hadn't taken offense. Truth was, he kind of liked it. The name implied strength and durability, attributes that Freeman believed he had in spades. So he'd let them have their fun and tried to perpetuate the legend by adopting an even more severe facial set, if that was possible.

But they hadn't meant it in fun. Freeman remembered that when he told Mr. Singer, "Yeah, I know them. And they're no friends of mine."

Well, it was pretty clear that Mr. Singer hadn't been

very thorough with his background check, because he didn't know Freeman at all. He should have talked to a few Mexicans back in Cuidad Obregon, who could have told him how Freeman tended to overreact when faced with ultimatums.

He started the car and pulled away from the curb, hung a left onto Hollywood and headed for the Eros and the little nurse, feeling good about himself and what he had planned for Mr. Super-Mouth Singer.

CHAPTER FIFTEEN

This time Caprita didn't even dare hope that it might be a maid unlocking the door, knowing it would be him, and she was right. He came in carrying the blue duffle bag that he took with him everywhere, placed it on the closet shelf, then walked to the bed unclasping his knife. She wished he would be less menacing about it instead of approaching her with that wide-eyed blank stare he always wore that never revealed his thoughts.

He cut her legs free and peeled the adhesive tape from her mouth. Was it her imagination, or was he more considerate this time? Seeing her as a person after all.

He picked up the cassette recorder, reversed the tape and carried it to his usual seat at the table. He pushed the PLAY button and set it down, turning to her again.

"You know something, foxy?" he said. "You're a good hostage. You've been very cooperative."

Caprita thought, *Oh, brother!*

"You really are. You don't snivel and whine and get all teary-eyed like most women would do in your situation. You don't ask for anything, except a drink of water or to go to the bathroom, and you do what you're told without too much protest."

"Thank you," she said, then immediately realized how silly that sounded.

"That leaves me a problem...what to do with you, because I've grown fond of you. Guess it's all that repressed affection and generosity bottled up inside me just screaming to come out, don't you figure?"

"I don't believe you're the type of man who commits random violence for no reason," Caprita said, voice even, stomach knotted. "You'll do the right thing when you see I'm no threat to you."

"Right twice, foxy. I appreciate that. Now, a lot of guys, they get a thrill out of being just plain mean to somebody for no cause whatsoever. Not me. You got to do something to me first. I also believe in being a gentleman, so I'm gonna give you a break."

"You won't be sorry," Caprita said. "And I still mean what I said about not going to the police, I swear you won't have to worry about that."

"Oh, I'm not worried," Freeman said, watching her closely. "You can't go to the police when you're dead."

The look that crossed her face was priceless, the way it went from expectation to dread in less than a heartbeat. Freeman photographed it with his mind for future reference, the way she licked her lips and tried to swallow before giving him a scared little smile.

"You're joking, right? Please don't do that, it makes me feel very uncomfortable."

"That's understandable," Freeman said reasonably. "Because it's no joke."

"But ... *why?* I thought you said you were going to let me go."

"I never said that. What I told you was I don't believe in unnecessary violence and I don't believe in being mean to somebody who's done me no harm. All that means is I'll be merciful when the time comes and make sure you don't suffer none. If you stop and think about it, that makes you a pretty lucky nurse. You don't want to know what I've got in mind for the others when they get here."

"Others?"

"Yeah. Gonna be having some company before long. Your boyfriend included."

"You talked to Allen?"

"Less than an hour ago. He thinks he's on the way to rescue you. Appears to me that—"

He paused and leaned closer to the cassette recorder, his interest captured by the minute sound of voices on the tape. They built in volume, then trailed off. Freeman relaxed and settled back in the chair. Caprita could have cried, she was so relieved. Then she wondered what she had to be so relieved about, and suddenly this track-switching of emotions was making her become unraveled.

"You *enjoy* this, don't you," she said, making it a statement and not a question. "Some warped part of your brain tells you committing terrorist acts against innocent people is *pleasurable.* I can't even *conceive* of a mind that perverted."

"Careful, foxy. I'm just beginning to like you."

"*Like me?* You don't even like yourself. But you defy description, mister whatever your name is. Unless it's sociopath."

She ran out of breath and looked away, realizing that she was on the edge of hysteria.

Freeman said, "You finished?"

She didn't answer.

Freeman got up and turned the light off in the kitchenette, then began slowly pacing the room, his shadow falling across Caprita each time he passed in front of the TV. She was more composed now, able to appreciate that she'd gone too far.

"So you think I'm a sociopath, huh?"

"Yes, goddamn you, I do." She was committed now. "Something made you that way. No one comes into this life programmed to just kill and inflict pain."

Freeman paused in front of the TV, his voice coming from a silhouette. "That's where you're wrong, little nurse. Everything's programmed. You have to have people like me, like you have to have wars, famine and pestilence. You have to keep a nice balance. So many wars, so many famines, so many plagues, so many people like me. That can't be left to chance, foxy, it's too important to planet survival. It's a lot like sex. After we come the first time, we're fucked." He almost cracked the start of a smile in that stone face. "So you see? Your argument's dead." He leaned on the last word.

He resumed his pacing as Caprita let her head fall back on the pillow, mentally and physically exhausted after not having slept in nearly two days. She needed to organize her thoughts and stop wasting time trying to affect him.

She had to find out about Allen.

"Then you're planning to kill Allen even if he does what you want?"

"Oh, I have special plans for him. He's bringing an old friend of mine. I've got plans for him, too." He made a turn and came back. "It's been a bad year for me, foxy. Eight months, actually. I had my house blown up, my boat blown up, lost a couple million dollars cash, the state of Arizona wanted to kill me, and my old friend frames me for murder. It can get to you."

He went into the bathroom and urinated with the door open, washed his hands carefully in the sink and came out drying them on a white towel.

"If you need to use the bathroom," he said, "better tell me now. I'll be going out again soon."

"You're bringing them there?"

"That's right, foxy. Me and my buddy and your boy-friend. Should be a nice reunion. So you'd better pee right now, 'cause this time I'll be leaving you a little less comfortable than I've done so far."

"I can't imagine—"

"You won't have to," he told her, "I'm about to show you."

CHAPTER SIXTEEN

He was up there all right, Cage was sure of that. Behind the wheel of the Cougar, parked in the lot across the driveway, he had a real clear view of the eighteenth floor and the wraparound balcony of PH–2.

It was dark up there now, a few minutes after two o'clock in the morning, but earlier the place had been lit up like a beacon. Cage had seen him through the lens of the twenty power Bushnells that rested on the passenger seat, had watched him moving around in the den like he was restless, sometimes with a cordless phone to his ear. Once, around ten-thirty he'd stepped out on the balcony wearing a T-shirt and checkered walking shorts and gazed out over the rail at the ocean, sipping from a cocktail glass. As he turned to go back inside, he'd looked down for a moment. Cage had focused the Bushnells and brought him in close enough to see that the worry lines had returned. Then he'd gone into the den, closing and presumably locking the sliding glass door, but leaving the drapes open halfway. Cage had lowered the binoculars and slumped down in the seat so he wouldn't get a crick in his neck, gearing himself for a long wait.

Now Cage picked up the binoculars and scanned the penthouse again, searching for signs of movement. There was none. The same for the entrances to the lobby and the underground garage, which were also visible from his vantage point. One car going in fifteen minutes ago, none coming out.

With the Timex/transponder on his wrist, ready to be activated, he had to glance at the digital clock on the dash to keep track of the time. It now read 2:16 A.M.

Time to go.

Cage had disconnected the dome bulb to minimize attention. He got out and closed the door quietly, adjusting the fanny pack around his waist that had HEAL THE BAY written across the pouch. He zipped his windbreaker over the thirty feet of thin nylon rope ladder wrapped around his body and did another quick sweep of the area. It was still clear.

He walked casually across the driveway to the locked door leading to the stairwell, inserted a thin strip of flexible steel shaped like an *S* into the crack behind the bolt guard, and gave a sharp tug. The bottom curve of the *S* slid between the latch plate and the bolt, depressing the spring for a fraction of a second and allowing him to pull the door open.

He took the stairs slowly, one at a time, conserving energy, sneakers now and again letting out hollow squeaks against the metal steps that echoed from the walls.

He paused on the penthouse landing and eased the door open, put his eye in the crack and surveyed the corridor. The guard was there, a different one from before. This one was white, maybe early fifties, tilted back against the wall in a straight back chair reading the L.A. *Times*. Large weapon on his hip that could have been a Magnum.

Cage let the door close and continued up two more flights, ignoring the sign on the wall that read NO ROOF ACCESS. The heavy door at the top was dead-bolted with a pretty good Corbin lock. He took a set of lock picks from the fanny pack, selected a rake and torque wrench and went to work on it.

Three minutes later he was on the half-roof, a low depression between the stairwell housing and the outer wall of PH–2. He stepped over the guard rail and made his way cautiously to the southwest edge, stretched out on his belly and peered over the lip.

The wraparound balcony was ten feet directly below, abutting the stairwell housing. Cage knew that it started outside the kitchen and ended at the dining room around the southeast corner. During his security inspection, this had been his greatest concern. Now he was grateful he'd had the chance to observe it.

He went back to the stairwell railing and unwrapped the nylon rope from around his body. He attached spring hooks to the two loops on one end and secured each to separate vertical rungs of the guard rail.

The lip of the roof was eight feet away. Cage played out the twin coils of nylon with interspersing rungs and dropped them over the edge. The ladder unraveled as it fell through the night past the balcony below and pulled up swaying in the breeze.

Cage got a good grip on the rope, squirmed around until he was hanging over the edge, and went down one rung at a time, concentrating on the smooth surface of the wall and blocking out the fact that he was suspended in space eighteen stories above the concrete.

He reached the balcony, swung over it and stood motionless in the shadows for several minutes. Then he moved to the sliding glass door that led to the kitchen, fished a pen light from the fanny pack and examined the area. The door was locked, as expected, and with the tiny beam from the penlight he could see that Hollister had also laid a broom handle in the track. The man was taking no chances on Freeman McKee getting his hands on him. He was prepared to hibernate up here for the duration.

Cage didn't bother trying to find an easier entrance. He wanted to go in through the kitchen. It was the farthest point from the upstairs bedrooms, lessening the possibility of being detected by the small amount of noise he would need to make.

He knelt by the door and went into the fanny pack again, this time coming out with a battery-powered high-speed drill the size of an electric toothbrush. The quarter-inch carbon bit was diamond-tipped and rotated at fifteen-hundred r.p.m.s, powered by a nine-volt booster-battery encased in a heavy cork handle. It was capable of boring through an eighth of an inch of solid steel plating with only a whisper of sound. Paul Banes had designed it, calling it his All Purpose Burglar Tool. Sometimes, he'd said, even honest people needed to make an illegal entry. Cage could identify with that.

He inspected the broom handle under the narrow beam from the penlight, then wetted his finger and marked a spot on the bottom of the glass that he figured was just about dead center. He positioned the drill bit accordingly and pressed the trigger.

It took the diamond bit revolving at super high

speed exactly eight seconds to crystalize a clean quarter-inch hole in the glass while barely making a sound. Cage inserted one of the slender spring steel lock picks through the hole, jiggled it around until he had it under the broom handle, then used leverage to roll it right out of the track, where it did a lazy turn and came to rest against a kitchen chair.

He stood and turned his attention to the door lock, which he already knew was a bolt-action instead of the standard latch kind, which meant he wouldn't be able to shim it. But with Paul's APBT, he drilled another hole slightly above the locking knob and used the S-shaped tool to turn it from the inside. Then, inch by inch, he opened the door until he was able to squeeze through and slide it closed behind him.

And just like that, he was in.

Now, then . . .

Ben Hollister was having a nightmare but didn't know it. It all seemed too real to him. He was wading through a quagmire, bogged down in gooey mud up to his waist, not getting anywhere. Behind him was Freeman McKee, who appeared to be hovering above the muck, closing in on him. He was holding a flaming armadillo that was making bloodcurdling squeals as the fire consumed it, extending the creature toward him as if it were a peace offering. Ben was in a frenzy, darting crazed looks over his shoulder at the apparition bearing down on him, flailing at the sucking mud that was holding him captive. McKee drew nearer, looming larger, lifting the blazing armadillo that was still making unearthly screeching sounds high above his head. He launched the burning animal at him and it flew straight for his face, causing Ben to let out his own scream and give a desperate lurch that yanked him free from the mud and sent him sprawling onto cool green grass that had a sweet freshness that he inhaled deeply into his lungs...only to have the scent instantly change into the stench of charred flesh that assaulted his nostrils, and then he saw that the flaming armadillo had transformed itself into a serene John Malone, who was standing over him all dressed in white, wearing a dignified expression. John was bending down to him now, his presence highlighted by a soft yellow light as he reached out a hand and gripped Ben's arm with a strength that surprised him, saying, "Get up, Ben, you're coming with me..."

Ben came awake with a start and tried to bolt upright in bed, but the fury behind the heel of Cage's hand as it slammed against his forehead caused him to crumple back onto the pillow, dazed. He was vaguely aware of his head being lifted, something cold and coarse being looped around his neck and drawn tight. The cobwebs were clearing now and he was squinting into the light from the bedside lamp at the distorted features of Allen Cage leaning over him, putting pressure on the clothesline noose around his neck.

"Now, do like I said," Cage told him. "One peep out of you trying to alert your man outside and I'll hang you from that balcony, you understand me, you sleazy bastard?"

"Oh, yeah, but...Jesus *Christ,* man, you can't—"

Cage stiff-armed him against the forehead again, not quite as hard as before but enough to get his attention.

"I can do anything I want with you, Ben, because now I know for sure I'm right. You're coming with me, and I really hope you put up a big argument so I can show you what an effort it is for me not to run you headfirst right through that window and listen to you yell all the way down. Now get up on your feet."

Cage jerked the line for emphasis, pulling Ben Hollister halfway out of bed. He made a choking sound and clutched the rope as he rolled onto the carpet and staggered to his feet. He wore nothing but white Jockey shorts a size too small for him. "Please ... please—"

"Shut up, Ben, and listen to me. I'm taking you out the same way I came in, and that's over the roof. There's a rope ladder outside the kitchen you're going to have to climb, so get used to the idea. And remember I'll be right behind you with a grip on this line, and I won't hesitate to let you splatter all over the driveway down there at the first funny move even if I have to go with you."

Ben was pleading with his hands and trying to pull the Jockey shorts out of the crack of his ass at the same time, saying, "Wait a minute, you're taking me to that fucking nut case, aren't you? You can't *do* that, goddamn it, he'll kill me—"

"Then he'll kill us both," Cage said, tying his end of the line tightly around his wrist, "because I'll be right there with you. So you'd better pray to God that you were right when you said I was your salvation. I'm all you're gonna have."

Cage gave the line another tug and led him out of the bedroom, down the stairs, through the den and into the kitchen, Ben pleading with him all the way, offering him money, anything he wanted, just don't take him to Freeman McKee. How about his clothes, he said, at least let him go and put some pants on. Cage finally told him to shut up and yanked him out onto the balcony.

Ben Hollister was having a hard time comprehending that this fucker was really taking him out of his penthouse condo on the eighteenth floor with a goddamn armed guard right outside the door. And here he was letting the guy have his way, leading him around by the neck like some jackass and not even trying to stop him. The guy didn't even have a *gun*, for God's sake. Then Ben saw that flimsy rope ladder the man wanted him to climb swinging and twisting in the warm breeze, and he thought, *What the fuck am I doing?*

Ben suddenly let go of the clothesline, shifted his feet and uncorked a roundhouse right that was meant to land flush on Cage's jaw and knock him into the middle of next week. But Cage, backpedaling toward the balcony railing, had been expecting some kind of play and saw it coming. He yanked on the line and at the same time took a half-step to the side. Ben was caught off balance in the middle of his swing, and his momentum spun him around a hundred and eighty degrees and sent him stumbling backward against the waist-high guardrail with such velocity that his upper body kept right on going and flipped him head over heels. For an instant he teetered there on the rail, a human seesaw fighting for equilibrium and a hand-hold. Then gravity won out and sent him slipping off into the night, so paralyzed with fear that all he could get past his constricted vocal cords was a startled, "Uhhh."

Cage reached for him a milisecond too late, then reflexes took over and he clamped his free arm around the guardrail and braced himself as best he could before Ben's weight coming to a sudden stop six feet past the balcony nearly sent him tumbling into space as well. The strain on his arm felt as if it were being torn from its socket. He bit his lip against the pain, managed to twine a leg around one of the vertical rails, and pulled. His injured shoulder only allowed him to lift Ben a few inches and no more. The man was hanging in air, turning from side to side with his

head tilted back and eyes bulging as he clung to the
rope with one hand and clawed at the noose that was
now pulled tight around his neck with the other. His
mouth was open, working like a beached fish, making
gargling noises.

Cage released his grip on the railing, trusting the
leverage from his anchored leg to keep him from going
over, used his other hand to help reel in Ben Hollister,
who by now was unconscious, arms hanging limp at
his sides.

Cage gave a final heave, putting his back into it,
and brought Ben's shoulders to within a few inches
of the railing. He reached down quickly with his good
hand, got it under the man's armpit, and on the count
of three gave it everything he had, thinking Caprita's
life depended on it, and pulled Ben Hollister's one-
hundred-and-seventy-six pounds of dead weight up
and over the railing, sending them both sprawling,
with Ben on top.

Cage pushed him off, rolled him onto his back and
loosened the noose. The man's face was turning purple, and his eyes were red from ruptured blood vessels,
but he was still breathing and he had a strong heartbeat. The noose had simply closed off the carotid artery and shut down the blood supply to his brain. If
he hadn't grabbed the line at the last second the way
he did, the fall would have broken his neck.

He'd be coming around in a few minutes. But before
he did, Cage wanted to get him off that balcony. He
swung Ben's arms over his sore shoulder and lifted
him in a fireman's carry, bounced him a couple of
times to distribute his weight evenly, then took hold
of the rope ladder with his free hand and swung his
leg over the railing.

He went up the ladder with a singleminded purpose
that refused to acknowledge pain or fatigue, keeping

Hollister balanced precariously over his shoulder while he took it a step at a time. He had him now, and nothing in the world was going to stop him from bringing the man to Freeman McKee.

He reached the half-roof quicker than expected and dumped Ben on the asphalt gravel while he hauled in the rope ladder, untied it, and stuffed the whole thing in an air-conditioning shaft. Then he went back to Hollister, picked him up and lugged him over the guardrail, through the roof door, dropped him again at the top of the landing.

Cage knelt and raised the man's eyelids. The pupils stared sightlessly up at him, refusing to dilate. He was still out of it. What to do? He sure as hell wasn't carting Ben Hollister down eighteen—make that twenty—flights of steps. And he'd ruled out the elevator from the beginning. For one, there was a twenty-four-hour-a-day doorman stationed in the lobby. For another, with a building this size, there was always the chance of someone getting on before they reached the lower level and exited through the garage, even at this hour. Which left him only one alternative.

Cage expanded the noose that still hung loosely from Hollister's neck, lifted his arms through and pulled it snug around his chest. He shortened up on the lead until he had the man's head and upper body several inches off the floor, then started down the stairs, dragging Ben beside him while keeping his head elevated high enough to prevent it from striking the metal steps as he skidded along on his back. His Jockey shorts hit a snag and ended up around his knees, then came the rest of the way off before he reached the next landing.

Ben was groaning now, fluttering his eyelashes, awareness coming back. Cage leaned over, backhanded him and the man's eyes came open.

"You with me now?" Cage said, and slapped him again. "Stand up and walk, goddamn it, or I'll drag you all the way to the bottom."

Ben struggled to his feet and stood there weaving with his head down, the fight gone out of him, either unmindful or uncaring about his nakedness.

"Move it," Cage said, and took up the slack on the line.

Ben went the rest of the way down on unsteady legs, using the wall for support, docile as a lamb and still in partial shock.

When they reached ground level Cage held the exit door open a crack and checked outside. Still quiet, nobody in sight. He opened it all the way and shoved Ben through.

"Run," Cage told him.

Ben lurched along beside him as Cage trotted across the lighted driveway and then into welcome shadow as they reached the Cougar parked in the back row. Ben was gasping now. He leaned against the car while Cage unlocked the passenger door and opened it.

"Inside," he said.

Ben eased into the passenger seat, moving like a sleepwalker. Cage leaned in and fastened the seatbelt around him.

"We're going for a ride, Ben," Cage said. "If you make any move to take that seatbelt off I'll tie you to the bumper and drag you. You with me?"

Ben stared at his lap without speaking.

Cage stepped back and closed the door...then heard a rustle of sound behind him just before a brilliant light exploded inside his head. He hit the pavement and did not move.

Freeman McKee put the spring-loaded sap back in his hip pocket and gave Cage a nudge with the shiny toe of his shoe. Out cold. He stepped over the body,

opened the passenger door and leaned in. Ben Hollister was still contemplating his lap.

"How you doing, Ben?" Freeman said. "You've been
a very bad boy lately."

Ben never lifted his head. He was still hanging by
the neck from the eighteenth floor, rushing toward that
white light from which there would be no return.

For the moment, there was no room in his heart for
additional fears.

CHAPTER SEVENTEEN

The jostling was driving away the fog, shaking him
from an opaque world into consciousness. Cage
opened his eyes. It was still dark, and at first he was
confused, wondering where he was and what had happened. It flashed in his mind that a security guard had
tipped in behind and cold-cocked him, but in the next
instant he realized that he was in the trunk of a moving car, and they didn't normally transport you to jail
that way. Moments later he realized he was in the
Cougar; he recognized the husky tone of the engine,
the rolled-up sleeping bag in the left corner that he
could touch with his foot.

McKee.

He'd been suckered again.

The thought was confirmed when he heard Ben Hollister's voice coming through the trunk, high-pitched
and whining, then McKee's telling him to shut up,
they'd talk when they got to the cabin. It sounded like
Ben had finally gotten over his shock.

Cage was on his side, knees drawn up and hands tied behind his back. It was a professional job, his palms turned outward to keep him from reaching the knots. His shoes were off, his belt was missing, and the Timex/transponder had been taken from his wrist.

So much for Larry's fine-tuned planning. He'd be at Zuma Beach right now, hidden in some cranny within a two-mile radius of the restrooms, warming up his receiver, and here he was stuffed in a trunk twenty miles away heading for who knew where. But he wasn't too concerned . . . as long as his little surprise hadn't been discovered.

Years ago, after he'd first gone to federal prison, an old-timer named Ronnie Harper had told him that the most versatile tool an enterprising con could carry that was practically undetectable was a sliver from one of those old-fashioned double-edged razor blades, like a Gillette, maybe an eighth of an inch wide.

"You can hide it anywhere," Ronnie Harper had told him, "between your fingers, up your nose, in your ass, if you wrap it in something first. Stick it between your toes or hide it in your pubic hair. You got a hundred places on your body where you can sneak it past shakedowns, even if they use a metal detector, 'cause it's below the sensitivity level they're set at." Cage had wanted to know what was so great about a piece of razor blade. Ronnie Harper had grinned and said, "Let me tell you what's so great about it. For one thing, it's perfect for shimming handcuffs—you just slide it down between the ratchet teeth and locking pin, put pressure on it and, presto mesto, the cuff opens. It's great for cutting key patterns out of melted-down toothbrushes for opening Folger/Adams security locks, which happen to be standard on just about every jail and prison in the country. It's thin enough and flexible enough to trip a knob lock, and if you've got enough time you can even cut through Plexiglas and Lexan, which the feds use in most of their metropolitan correctional centers. Add to that the obvious stuff, such as making weapons, cutting rope, or cutting throats, and you've got something with the potential to get you out of a lot of tights. That little piece of steel is only limited by your imagination, my friend. So go imagine."

Cage had remembered the advice, even had opportunity to put it to use on occasion. Now he was hoping to call on it again.

He rubbed his forearm lightly against one of the belt loops at the back of his pants, searching for the tiny strip of razor blade he'd sewn into the material that afternoon and practiced with for five hours until he had it stabilized just right; the cutting edge facing outward with only a thin piece of cloth covering the blade. He was betting that Freeman McKee would follow the pattern he was most comfortable with when restraining his victims. All Cage would have to do was rub the twine against that belt loop and the brand-new Wilkinson Sword blade would take care of the baling twine. And judging by the coarse texture of his bonds, that's what the man had used. Cage was confident it would work, if McKee didn't kill him first.

Except, try as he might, he couldn't feel the razor-sharp edge of the blade anywhere.

Though Freeman didn't show it, he could appreciate humor as well as the next man, and he was having a good time with Ben Hollister sitting buck-ass naked in the passenger seat, hands tied behind his back in the same way as Cage. Telling him how it was strange the way a man's pecker and balls just shriveled up to nothing when he was filled with the fear of God. Look at him, he said, couldn't see nothing but pubic hair. But on the other hand, it was stranger yet how a man's pecker would swell to three times its normal size in death. Kind of a waste, wasn't it? Just when you couldn't use it.

Freeman drove through the night with one hand on the wheel and the other lightly stroking his thigh, his only outward sign of anticipation. Now and again he would turn his head to Ben Hollister, who was squirming around and wetting his lips, trying to think of something to say while he looked for a police car, and if he saw one he was going to jam his foot on the accelerator and keep it there, that's how desperate he was.

"You know something," Freeman said, "it's really a miracle what happened up there on that balcony. I was scared to death you weren't gonna make it." He shook his head in mock-wonder, searching for an on-ramp to the Santa Monica Freeway. "Fate, that's what it was. You just weren't meant to go that way. See, I picture something entirely different for somebody like you. You're what they call a real dynamic kind of guy, and I see you going out in a real dynamic way. You believe in destiny?"

Ben, thoroughly spooked, started gushing, saying he'd make it worth Freeman's while if he'd let him go.

"I got money," Ben told him. "Big money. I can make you a very wealthy man, Freeman, you'll never have to work another day in your whole life, and I mean cash money, you just name it ... Oh, *Jesus* ..."

Ben leaned forward and rested his forehead on the padded dash. After a moment his shoulders began to heave.

Freeman pretended to think about it as he turned onto Lincoln Boulevard. Then he said, "Naw, I don't think so. Besides, what I do isn't work."

Ben pounded his head against the dash.

"Tell you what I would like, though," Freeman said.

Ben kept his eyes on the dash. "What?"

"I've sure taken a shine to that earring."

"Shit, man, then *take* it," Ben said quickly, and leaned toward him.

Freeman said "thanks" and with a speed Ben wouldn't have believed possible, reached out and grabbed the earring and yanked with such force that the post tore right through the ear lobe.

Ben screamed and pressed the wounded ear against his shoulder.

Freeman dropped the earring into his coat pocket and said, "Shut up, you don't even know the meaning of pain, yet."

Ben moaned and let his head fall against the seat back. "Why are you doing this? What do you want, the Duracon-L? That's what Cage said."

"For starters."

"Well, all this isn't necessary, all you had to do was ask. You don't even have to do that, just pick up a back copy of Business Week. The whole chemical breakdown is listed there. Jesus, Freeman, you tore my fucking ear off, man."

"What did you say?"

"My ear, it's bleeding like shit, it feels—"

"I mean about Duracon-L," Freeman said. "What's this about the chemical breakdown being in a magazine?"

"It is, I swear it. Ask Cage. I even gave him a copy." Ben was swinging his head again, looking for a non-existent police car, all of them at Dunkin' Donuts when they were supposed to be out on the streets protecting innocent people from lunatics like Freeman McKee...oh, Christ, he was getting on the freeway. So much for that.

A lot had gone through Freeman's mind over a few short seconds. Hollister knew better than to piss him off even more than he already was by telling him a lie that could easily be checked. So assume he's telling the truth. What did that say about Mr. Singer, the man who was paying him fifty grand to learn a secret that had been published in a magazine? Was he that dumb? Freeman didn't think so, the way he'd been so careful about everything up till now. The man was paying for his expertise and didn't owe him any explanations. But he didn't owe him any lies, either. Freeman was very suspicious about people who lied to him for no reason. It usually meant they were going to try to fuck you one way or another. If that was Mister James Bond-Singer's plan, he was in for an eye-opener.

But then there went his twenty-five grand that he was willing to settle for in order to work on the man. And he was nearly flat broke.

Freeman said, "Ben, how much money is your life worth to you?"

Ben reacted like he'd just been told he won the lottery. "Everything I got, every dime. I'll get you a cashier's check soon as the bank opens. How about that?"

Freeman settled into the number-two lane of the nearly deserted freeway, eased the Cougar up to an even fifty-five and kept it there. He said, "How much are we talking about, Ben? Don't lie to me now. I don't like being lied to."

Ben did some quick figuring in his head, deciding how much he could reasonably hold back. "Close to a hundred thou," he said. That sounded like a nice even number. "That's cash, now, without having to liquidate or borrow anything."

He blew a drop of sweat from his nose and waited for Freeman's reply, wondering if he'd cut it too close, and was all set to tell him he'd plain forgot about that forty thousand dollar CD account—

"A hundred grand, huh?"

"Give or take a thousand or two. No problem."

"Then you just bought yourself a pardon, old buddy," Freeman said. "Ain't it great the way capitalism works?"

CHAPTER EIGHTEEN

Caprita was on her stomach, secured hand and foot by the rough baling twine that ran from her ankles to her wrists, then up and around her neck, feeling like every vertebra in her spine had snapped. It was a frightful position, one that could very easily strangle her if she struggled too much.

She tensed at the sound of a car making its way slowly up the driveway. Headlights flashed through the closed drapes as it parked outside the door, briefly illuminating the room before they went out. It was the first time he'd ever parked in front of the unit, preferring to sneak up on her without warning and listen at the door before entering. She knew he did. There had been times when she'd actually sensed him out there, lurking like a peeping Tom, and even now the knowledge made her skin crawl.

She suddenly raised her head and listened intently to the deep rumble of the engine that was still idling outside. Something very familiar about it.

And then she recognized Allen's Cougar, not a doubt in her mind, Oh, God, it was him, it was really *him*. She threw her head back and screamed through her nostrils, a long wail that expressed her terror in ways that words never could.

The engine shut off and she listened again, hearing the soft thud of car doors closing, unhurried footsteps on the gravel. Then reality brought her back to earth and she remembered what the man had promised the night before. It might be Allen's car. But he would be as much a prisoner as she was.

Caprita tilted her head as a naked man stumbled in through the door with his hands bound behind his back. The left side of his face was streaked with blood and his body was scraped and bruised. He was just as surprised to see her, and he pulled up short and tried to turn his back, but Freeman was right behind him, closing the door and herding him to a corner of the room.

"Sit down," Freeman told him.

"Sure, Freeman, anything you say," Ben said, and used the wall to slide to the floor. He gazed around the room, met Caprita's eyes and nodded, "How you doing?"

"Don't move from that spot or it's back to plan A," Freeman said, and left the room.

Caprita kept her attention on the open door, knowing who would be coming in next. She listened to the trunk being raised, heard the man say "hurry up." Then the trunk closed and footsteps approached... and there he was, coming through the doorway and pausing when he saw her lying there. He was bound, but he didn't appear damaged, and Caprita was glad that she didn't have to see him beaten and bleeding like the other man. That would have sent her over the edge for sure. She greeted him with sad eyes and shook her head in silent apology.

Cage looked at her and felt overwhelming relief to find her alive when all along, he had to admit it now, he never thought he would. Then his mood changed at the way she was being restrained, the strip of tape covering her mouth, the small bruise on the side of her face. He turned to McKee, who was just closing the door behind him.

Cage said, "Is that necessary?"

"You mean having her tied up like that? What kind of question is that for a smart clown like you to ask?"

"What about the bruise?"

"Oh, that." Freeman opened his coat to show the handle of the .22 sticking out of his waistband. "Guess me and foxy here got a little carried away. Now get over there next to the bed and lie down on the floor. On your belly."

Cage did and managed to give Caprita a look as he sank to the floor and rolled over on his stomach. He couldn't be sure, but he thought that her eyes signaled that she understood.

Freeman went to the closet and removed the blue duffle bag from the top shelf, set it on the floor and began rummaging through it. He took out a fresh roll of heavy baling twine, went back to Cage and knelt over him.

"Seeing you're so fascinated with the way your little nurse is all laced up, I'll just give you a demonstration of what it's like."

He placed a slipknot around Cage's wrists, drew it tight, looped the twine several times around his neck, pulled his head back, then ran the lead between the slipknot at his wrists down to his ankles and secured the end with a double half hitch.

He patted Cage on the buttocks and stood. "There, how's that feel?"

Cage didn't answer. He was concentrating on the razor-blade sliver he'd finally located. It must have twisted out of position when McKee took his belt off. Now it was lying flat inside the belt loop instead of edgewise. It would be more difficult, and he'd probably cut himself in the process, but it could still be done. If McKee would just take those eerie blue eyes off him for maybe three straight minutes. Make that two. Cage was ready to cut his hands off and beat the man to death with the stumps if that's what it took.

"I see you're still a tough guy," Freeman said. "Good. Wimps are no fun."

He studied Caprita a moment, then reached down and ripped the tape from her mouth. "I heard you out there, foxy," he said mildly. "What did I tell you would happen if you tried a stunt like that?"

"I was choking," she said between gasps.

"Sure you were. I'll have to show your macho boy-friend I'm a man of my word. So think about what I told you I was gonna do and try to guess when I'm gonna do it. You like to analyze so much, analyze that."

He held her gaze until she looked away, then shifted his attention to Cage. "I don't want you two talking to each other, you hear me?"

"We hear you."

"Good. 'Cause we might have a little time to kill before the fun starts, and I think it would be a fine idea if my old pal Ben Hollister fessed up to why he took out his partner like he did. What about that, Ben? Don't you agree confession's good for the soul?"

Ben said, "Hey, wait a minute, I thought we were together here."

"Wrong. All we have is a business arrangement to

let you stay alive. It doesn't mean I like you and it damn sure doesn't mean I forgive you for railroading me and making me out to be some kind of freak who gets off chopping up monkeys. I want you to confess your sins in front of these good witnesses and tell us what was so urgent about killing John Malone. Don't worry, they're not gonna tell anybody."

Ben cleared his throat and saw Caprita glaring at him.

"Make her stop looking at me like that," Ben said. "She's making me nervous."

Caprita turned her head without being told, intuition telling her the little jackal sitting on the floor was the root of this evil.

"Go ahead, Ben," Freeman said. "We're all ears."

Seeing he wasn't getting out of it, Ben took on an offended tone. "Duracon-L was *my* discovery," he said. "Four miles ahead of Silicon, a guaranteed moneymaker and instant recognition in high technology. I bring John Malone in, make him a partner because I need the capital so bad, and next thing you know he's a multimillionaire getting equal credit."

Cage was maneuvering his wrists against the belt loop, trying to find the cutting edge.

"You'd think he'd be grateful," Ben said, actually warming to it, "splittin' everything fifty-fifty when the only thing he was contributing was his name on the letterhead. But no, he couldn't let it go at that. He has to get bored and decide to make an exercise tape wearing gold tights and a monkey doing pushups on his back. I saw one of the demo cuts, and I swear to God it looked exactly like that monkey was fucking him."

"Bad for your reputation," Freeman said.

"Exactly. The sonofabitch was gonna distribute it under the BenJohn logo. Thirty minutes of filmed erotica with a capuchin monkey? We'd have been the laughing stock of the industry."

Ben hung his head at the painful memory, the perfect picture of a man who had been severely wronged. Convinced of it.

"That's a killing offense, all right," Freeman said. "But cutting a monkey's head off and sticking it on a gear shift, that's sick, Ben." He walked around the foot of the bed and sat down facing Hollister. "Of course, it was a little added incentive knowing you were gonna have BenJohn's all to yourself, wasn't it?"

"Well, what right did he have to live off my sweat the rest of his life? Then I go to him and say, John, you can't use the logo on your exercise tape, you'll run us out of business. He turns all huffy, telling me he owns half of it, and after that there was no reasoning with him."

Cage felt a sharp twinge in the soft flesh behind his left wrist bone and knew he'd found it. He forced his hands upward, feeling his way until he was pretty sure he had the twine resting against the razor edge that was eating its way out of his belt loop. Straining his neck to keep Freeman in view, he slowly began to saw.

Freeman was saying, "I bet you never would've had the nerve to do it if I hadn't shown up, would you, Ben? But I was a tailor-made patsy. Pretty cold, old buddy."

Ben nearly smiled. "Well, damn, Freeman, you didn't exactly come here to do me any favors yourself." He tried the smile again and this time it worked. "But that's business, right? Neither one of us ought to take it personally."

"Yeah, that's a good attitude," Freeman said, and turned to Cage. "Hey, clown. Did my man here give you a magazine that had this Duracon-L formula in it?"

Cage froze, stared at the wall, hoping he hadn't left a blood trail.

"That's right."

"What magazine?"

"Business Week."

Freeman looked at Ben. "Just checking. Can't be too careful these days."

He stood, picked up the duffle bag and went into the bathroom, leaving the door partially open.

Cage took the opportunity to continue his sawing, putting more vigor into it while McKee was temporarily out of sight. He heard a small gasp and realized that Caprita, from her elevated position on the bed, had seen him. He stared at the wall in fierce determination and didn't waste time responding. It was enough that she knew.

Freeman came out of the bathroom and dropped the duffle bag back on the floor. He stood there brushing at the wrinkles in his tan suit, then moved to the TV and sorted through the channels until he found CNN. He turned the sound up a little, swiveled the TV so it faced the table and sat down, easing the chair back on two legs.

"Okay," he said, "from here on out, nobody talks. I got some thinking to do. That goes for you too, Ben, confession's over. Don't you feel a lot better?"

Ben shook his head.

"Well, don't worry about it. Meditate a while, always helps. Think what a lucky man you are that I've got such a generous disposition. That's a side of me your friends here aren't gonna be seeing."

Ben said, "Hey, Freeman, can I have a pair of pants or something?"

"Don't have any pants."

"What about Cage, can I have his? Hell, he's not gonna need 'em. Come on, Freeman, I'm naked as a jaybird here."

Freeman glanced at Cage and Caprita, both stiff as boards and hardly daring to breathe. Good. Give them something to meditate about too.

"Later," Freeman said. He turned to the TV and watched Catherine Crier report on the state of the world.

Waiting for Mr. Singer and his twenty-five thousand dollars.

Cage was getting more agitated. They might really die in this secluded adult motel that he never even knew existed until now. McKee was sitting directly behind him with an unobstructed view of his hands. The guy was calm and relaxed as he listened to the news, and every now and then he would look at them, making it impossible for Cage to work. He was sweating freely now, beginning to ache from the constant strain on bone and muscle. It had to be torture for Caprita, who had been suffering far longer than he.

Come on, you bastard, Cage thought. *Move.*

Somebody tapped on the door knob, metal against metal.

Cage was amazed how fast Freeman McKee came to his feet, without effort or wasted motion. He faced the door like he was ready for combat, poised and loose, hand hovering close to the handle of the .22 sticking from his waist band.

Tapping again. Louder.

Freeman went to the door and stood to one side. "Who is it?"

The familiar voice said, "Mr. Singer."

Freeman opened the door.

He was a big man in a gray suit, partially in shadow,

but the .45 automatic in his hand was part of him that was in the light, the first thing that Freeman saw and the last thing he expected.

"Hello, Freeman," Joe Odell said. "Been dunking any heads in toilets lately?"

CHAPTER NINETEEN

Freeman backed slowly into the room, keeping his hand away from the .22 that he didn't stand a chance of reaching. Oh, he recognized Joe Odell, all right, he'd know that hog head anywhere. Only now the jowls dropped like a Saint Bernard and he'd put on about a hundred pounds since he'd last seen him in the boys' room with his head stuck in the shitter. Freeman felt no surprise and no fear; he'd already decided it was a good chance he was the prime target, anyway, ever since he'd learned about that magazine piece. That had been fate too, or he never would have gotten suspicious of Mr. Singer.

Joe Odell followed him into the room, closed the door and leaned against it. He seemed puzzled to find Cage and Caprita there, and he moved the .45 in a slow arc between them and Freeman McKee, who had stopped in the middle of the room and was watching Joe Odell. The guy had really grown—he stood about six-five and weighed at least two-seventy, most of it around his middle.

Ben Hollister had been gawking at Odell. "Well I'm a sonofabitch," he said, "it *is* you. I've never been so happy to see anybody in my whole life. Cut me loose, Joe, all these fuckers are tryin' to rob me."

"Shut up, Ben...McKee, who are these people?"

"Somebody who got in the way," Freeman said. "I don't suppose you brought my money, did you?"

"Oh, that's a great question," Joe Odell said. "Sure, I did, got it right in my pocket. Now use your left hand and real easy-like pull that pistol out of your waistband and toss it in front of me."

Freeman hesitated, then complied, his motions slow and deliberate. He never took his eyes off Joe Odell, who picked up the .22 and studied it.

"Silencer, huh? Real thoughtful of you." He sidestepped his way to the bed, keeping both weapons trained on Freeman McKee, and gave Cage and Caprita a brief inspection. "What are your names?"

"I'm Allen Cage and this is my fiancée Caprita Arciaga. And we'd be damn grateful if you'd untie us."

"I'm sure you would," Odell said. "But Mr. McKee here has put me—and you—in a position where I can't do that. Now you can identify me."

Cage looked up into the face of the man Freeman McKee had humiliated as a boy, and he didn't like what he saw. If vengeance wore a mask, it would look like Joe Odell.

Ben Hollister was confused. He said, "What the fuck's goin' on here, Joe?"

"I'll tell you what's going on," Freeman said quietly. "Mr. *Singer's* got a bad case of lost manhood. It's hung with him all these years. Given him nightmares, taken his self-respect, driven him to booze and pills and therapy. It's warped his little mind till he can't think of anything except settling the score. You went through a whole lot of trouble and expense setting this gig up, Joe. I hope it's worth it."

"Oh, it'll be worth it," Joe Odell said. "It's the only way I'll ever have any peace of mind. But not for the reasons you think."

Ben said, "Jesus Christ, if it bothers you so much, Joe, go ahead and shoot him. But, hey, *I* didn't do anything to you."

"You certainly didn't do anything to help me, either. None of you did, not you, or John Malone, or Paul Stanlowe, or Jessie White. You just stood there and let a kid who never hurt anyone be treated worse than a dog, and you never lifted a finger to help."

"Jesus, Joe—"

"Oh, I kept track of you, Ben. You and Malone were easy, all I had to do was read the papers. I knew where all of you had gone. Everybody but our gypsy friend Freeman. Then, what do you know, he drops right into my lap and I find out he's a full-blown homicidal maniac to boot. Can't you appreciate the irony of having Freeman working for me to get you three together all in one spot? Except for John Malone, of course. I don't know which one of you boys killed him, but I appreciate whoever it was saving me the trouble. After all, I'm no Freeman McKee."

Cage was sawing again, slowly. Very shortly Joe Odell was going to kill Freeman McKee and Ben Hollister. Then he was going to kill him and Caprita. The man wasn't going to leave any witnesses.

"But don't get the idea that I'm doing this only for revenge," Joe said. "It just happens to be a bonus."

He backed away from the bed and eased his bulk into the straight chair Freeman had been sitting in. He sighed, stretched out his legs but kept both guns trained on the center of Freeman McKee's chest.

"It might surprise you boys to know I'm a state senator now, have been for two years. Arizona, my adopted state after you made me ashamed to show my face in Texas, Freeman. I went and made something of myself . . . not like you, Ben, stealing from an employer by putting his time, knowledge and equipment to your own personal use."

"I *developed* that process through my own sweat, the court agreed with me—"

"The court said there was insufficient evidence to *prove* that you developed it on company time. There's a difference, Ben. Well, never mind. The *point* of all this is my career. You two, along with John Malone, could have ruined it for me. The other two who were in the toilet that day are dead, one in a plane crash, the other on military maneuvers in the Middle East."

Cage was sawing harder now, could taste the tension in the room. By craning his head to the left he could see Joe Odell slouched in the chair, a gun in each hand, facing Freeman McKee standing ten feet away. He was aware of Caprita's uneven breathing from close above and knew that she was still watching. And praying.

"So you're the only ones left," Joe Odell said. "Potential problems for my very promising future. But not after today."

Ben said, "What the hell kind of problem could I be to your career? That doesn't even make sense, Joe."

"Think about it. I happen to be very popular with my constituents back home. I defeated a veteran incumbent with sixty-two percent of the vote. I've got influence and financing behind me, and there's a move under way to have me run for Congress next year."

Ben licked his lips. "Okay, so?"

"Running for national office gives a candidate national exposure. He gets on network news, does sound-bites, holds press conferences. Millions of people get to know his face, and with a little luck he gets to be a household name."

Cage felt a sharp pain at the base of his wrist and thought he heard Caprita draw a quick breath. Now he'd done it. Went and cut himself. Nothing left except go all out and hope to work free before someone noticed the trickle of blood he had to be leaving behind. He bore down harder... *come on, come on, give*...

"Imagine how all those supporters would feel," Odell was saying, "If one of you boys went to the *Enquirer* or *Globe* and told them how Big Joe let some kid half his size stick his head in a toilet and not do anything about it, just lay there on the floor and bawl. And then sneaked out of town with his tail between his legs. That kind of thing could kill whatever I'd built up, ruin my whole career. Especially since one day I figure I may even decide to take a shot at the White House. Now do you understand, Ben? With you and Freeman out of the way, the thing never happened. It was just a nasty rumor someone started. Get the picture?"

Cage felt something pop and the twine binding his hands went slack.

"Yeah," Ben said. "I get the picture, but goddamn, Joe, you're going overboard here. We were *kids*. Nobody would hold that against you even if it did come out. I'd love to see you Senator or President or whatever the hell and be able to brag about how I know you—"

"Of course you would," Joe Odell said. "That also influenced my decision. But you're wrong about it not being held against me. Nobody wants to vote for a coward, Ben, and that's what I was. You think Jack Kennedy would have been elected President if anything like that ever come out about him? *PT–109* did it for him as much as his old man's money. That kind of thing has a way of sticking with you."

Odell looked at Freeman, who still hadn't moved or taken his eyes off him. "How about it, Freeman? Still want to coax that information out of Ben for me?"

Freeman didn't say anything.

Odell smiled. "That was another nice touch. A red herring, I think it's called. Disguise your real purpose with a fake one."

Cage had been waiting for a little circulation to come back into his fingers. Now he inched his hands out of the loose coils of twine, trying to keep the line running from his ankles to his neck from tightening. He flexed his fingers and felt for the razor-blade sliver in his belt loop.

"As you've gathered by now, Freeman, I don't have any interest in Ben Hollister's formula. But I did promise to let you have him, and I'll keep my word. So go ahead. Kill him. Do it with your bare hands, you sadistic sonofabitch, you enjoy it so much. *Do it.*"

"Hey, wait a fuckin' minute—"

"Shut up, Ben." Joe Odell was near trembling now, both guns wavering as he kept them centered on Freeman's chest. "You heard me. Go over there, Freeman, and do what you do best. And then I'm going to shoot you down like the sick animal you are with your own gun and nobody will ever hear a sound."

There was a moment of silence except for the muted sound of the television, a commercial for AT&T promising to reconnect returning customers free of charge.

Cage had the razor blade now, holding it between thumb and forefinger. Watching the scene while he waited for the right moment.

"You're gonna have to do all your own killing,"

Freeman said quietly. "I don't work for you anymore. Personally, I don't think you got the nerve to do it."

"Is that a fact?"

Ben had heard enough. He panicked and tried to get to his feet.

Joe Odell took deliberate aim with the .22 and pulled the trigger. There was a sound like a faint cough and plaster splattered from a hole in the wall two inches to the right of Ben Hollister's bobbing head. Another cough and a small red depression appeared next to his left nipple. Ben yelped and gazed dumbfounded at the wound, then slid back to a sitting position and stared sightlessly at nothing.

Cage marveled again at Freeman McKee's speed. His right hand jerked, then shot forward in an underhand toss and a double-blade knife whistled through the air and penetrated the right side of Joe Odell's neck an instant after he fired the second shot. He dropped the .45 and staggered a few steps away, clutching the knife, pulling it free in a spurt of blood that came from the severed carotid artery.

Freeman watched the dying man, keeping his distance as Odell did a slow dance around the room, trying to plug the hole in his neck. After a few moments he dropped the .22 and went down hard next to the dresser. He rested there on one elbow with both hands pressed against the wound.

Freeman picked up the .45 and walked to the dresser. He looked down at Joe Odell, watched the man's face losing color as he lost the fight to keep his lifeblood from escaping. Freeman thumbed back the hammer and took a shooting stance, legs apart, arm extended, and aimed at a spot in the middle of the man's forehead.

"Senator," he said, "you're no Jack Kennedy." And pulled the trigger.

The steel-jacketed slug entered Joe Odell's forehead between his eyes with sufficient force to bounce his head from the carpet. The explosion made Freeman's ears ring and filled the air with cordite, and so he never heard Cage move in behind him until he felt a searing pain between his legs that took his breath away and sent him rising up on his toes and spinning around. He still held the gun, but reflex had sent his hands scurrying to protect his groin.

Cage kicked him again, this time in the solar plexus, and Freeman grunted and let go of the gun. He went to his knees with his mouth working for air, trying to cover himself.

"I see you can change expression after all," Cage said. He stepped in and launched an uppercut from the floor that caught Freeman on the chin and sent him sprawling on his back. Cage straddled him and began to pound his fists into the man's face—left and right, left and right, putting his shoulder into each blow until his arms got tired and his knuckles ached and he finally heard Caprita screaming his name.

He rolled to his knees and stood and looked down at Freeman McKee. The man's features were unrecognizable. The nose was smashed, the lips flattened and split. His eyes were swollen closed and he bled from more than a dozen cuts. But, amazingly, he was still conscious and aware. He squinted at Cage. His upper lip had been cut so that he seemed to be giving him a bloody grin.

"You can kill me now, clown," he whispered. "It's finished. Can't you see it? I thought it was Hollister and Malone, but it was Joe Odell all the time. It started with him and it ends with him. Just like it was meant to be. Ask your woman what she thinks about destiny now..."

He broke into weak coughs while Cage picked up

the stained throwing knife, went to the bed and cut Caprita loose. She let her head and legs fall heavily to the bed while Cage stroked her hair and watched Freeman McKee. After a moment she reached up and took his wrist and squeezed it with a strength he never imagined she had.

"You all right?" he asked.

"I am now," she said into the pillow, and let go her grip on his wrist. "Please get me out of here." She looked at McKee. "Don't kill him, Allen, not like this."

"I'll be right back," he told her.

"You have to kill me," Freeman was saying. "You don't have a choice...neither of us do. You can't change destiny."

Cage just looked at him, shook his head, then moved to the open duffle bag on the floor, took out the roll of baling twine and knelt down beside McKee. He rolled him over onto his stomach, twisted his hands behind his back so the palms were facing outward, and secured them firmly.

"Destiny? I'll tell you what your *destiny's* gonna be, you sonofabitch," Cage said, and looped the twine over the man's ankles, pulling them up tight and feeding the line around his wrists and up to his neck. "You're gonna spend the rest of your unnatural life in a five-by-eight on the psych unit in Vacaville."

Cage wrapped two double-strands of twine around Freeman's neck, pulled his head back by the hair, then brought the end back down to his wrists and tied it off with two cinch knots.

"Whenever you come out of your cell it's gonna be in handcuffs and leg irons and escorted by a pair of correctional officers just dying to use their billy clubs on your ugly head. You'll get an hour a day recreation inside a wire cage with a couple other nut cases that you'll have to keep your eye on every second, because if they get set off for any reason they'll kill you quick. You'll be given medication to make you sleep, medication to keep you awake, and at the first little hint of aggression they'll hit you with a shot of Prolixin that'll turn you into a salivating zombie for a week. In your case you won't have far to go."

Cage checked the restraints and was satisfied they would hold. He stood and looked down at Freeman McKee, saw his bloodied features twisted in a grimace of pain. And something else.

Fear.

"Kill me," Freeman managed to get out. "It has to end this way—"

"It'll end the way I want it to end," Cage said. "It'll be my decision. Not your bullshit destiny's. Unless the State of California decides to execute you, which isn't likely, you're gonna be listening to crazies even worse off than you until the day you die. *That's* the way it was meant to be."

Cage went to Caprita, who was sitting now on the edge of the bed rubbing her wrists while she surveyed the horror around her as if she were in a dream. It looked like a scene out of "Helter Skelter."

Cage took her by the arm. "Hey. It's over. Let's get out of here."

She leaned against him as she got up from the bed. "What about them?"

"I'll dial 911 at the first pay phone and leave it for the cops and FBI to clean up."

Neither of them had a watch, but Cage estimated the time to be somewhere between three-thirty and four.

"Come on," he said. "We have to get to Zuma Beach."

On the way out Cage held the door and gave one last look at Freeman McKee, the man Ben Hollister and John Malone had called Stoneface. Those icy blue eyes had retreated now behind his swollen lids and were no longer visible. But he still wore that bloody grin.

Cage closed the door.